Luke ... made ...

"What experience do you have in running an airline—or any other business for that matter?" Luke didn't attempt to hide the derision in his voice.

"None whatsoever," Mike managed to answer calmly. She was perfectly aware of her lack of experience, but if he thought she was going to be intimidated, openly admit to her own doubts and anxieties, he'd be disappointed.

"I'm not a prospective employee. I'm your partner," she reminded him sweetly. "Equal partner," she added for good measure.

She saw a muscle clench along his jaw. "And how long do you think it'll be before the novelty of playing businesswoman of the year wears off?"

Mike looked at him with large thoughtful eyes. "We'll have to see, won't we?" she murmured serenely.

ROSEMARY GIBSON was born in Cairo, where her father was in the Foreign Service. She spent her childhood in Egypt, Greece and Vietnam, returning to England at the age of eight. Though she took teacher's training at Christ Church College, her working experience has been varied—community-service worker, barmaid, gas-pump attendant, and ground hostess and receptionist for an airline in Bournemouth, where she first started writing seriously. She began with short stories for various women's magazines before becoming a romance novelist. She lives in New Forest with her dog, Cindy, and a black cat called Jellybean.

Books by Rosemary Gibson

HARLEQUIN PRESENTS
1403—TO TRUST A STRANGER

ROSEMARY GIBSON

an unequal partnership

Harlequin Books

TORONTO • NEW YORK • LONDON
AMSTERDAM • PARIS • SYDNEY • HAMBURG
STOCKHOLM • ATHENS • TOKYO • MILAN
MADRID • WARSAW • BUDAPEST • AUCKLAND

Harlequin Presents first edition July 1992
ISBN 0-373-11474-5

Original hardcover edition published in 1991
by Mills & Boon Limited

AN UNEQUAL PARTNERSHIP

CHAPTER ONE

'Mr Duncan has arrived, Miss Harrington.'

'Thank you, John.' Michaelia looked up from the walnut desk, pen poised in her hand, and smiled at the stiffly erect, silver-haired man standing in front of her. Until five weeks ago, she remembered wistfully, she had simply been Miss Mike. But now John had evidently decided that the strictly formal address was more befitting to the new mistress of Rakers' Moon. 'Would you show him into the morning-room, please?'

She glanced at her gold wristwatch as John departed from the study. Luke Duncan was fifteen minutes early for their appointment. Unhurriedly, she finished the letter she was writing and sealed it in an envelope. There were letters of condolence still arriving and she was determined to answer each one personally.

She rose to her feet and smoothed the crease-resistant oatmeal linen dress over her hips and crossed the room, moving silently on the thick Persian rugs. She was well above average height, but even as a child had never been gawky, had controlled her long, slender limbs with a natural athletic grace. Her short, wilful curls had been temporarily subdued this morning, smoothed to her head in a silken, gleaming copper cap. Light make-up concealed the band of tiny freckles that dusted the high cheekbones and neat, straight nose; coral lip gloss outlined the perfectly curved mouth.

She walked the length of the long, tiled hall and opened the door to the morning-room, her eyes instantly drawn to the grey-suited figure standing by the window overlooking the cobbled courtyard, the spring sunshine glinting in his thick dark hair.

'Mr Duncan.' Mike extended a manicured hand and felt the pressure of strong, lean fingers against her own. Tilting her head, she looked directly into his face, absorbing the aggressively male features, the hard mouth that looked uncomfortable smiling and the dark grey eyes that were assessing her with cool detachment. Assessing her, she realised immediately, as if she were a complete stranger. There was no flicker of recognition in those cold eyes. Neither was there any trace of the appreciation she was accustomed to witnessing in male eyes.

'I was very sorry about your grandfather, Miss Harrington. I was in Sydney when I learned of his death, otherwise I should have liked to have attended the funeral.' He paused and added quietly, 'I both liked and respected Matthew a great deal.'

'Thank you,' she murmured, dark lashes dropping over her hazel eyes. Her grief was very personal and private, not something for public display. She'd been shocked to discover after his death that Matthew Kingston, her maternal grandfather, had been advised over a year ago by his medical practioner to retire and start taking life at a more leisurely rate. It was advice Matthew had refused to heed, his neglect culminating in that last fatal heart attack.

'Do sit down, Mr Duncan.' Mike indicated a well-worn leather armchair, and sat down gracefully into its matching counterpart, elegantly crossing her long, slim legs. 'I hope you had a pleasant flight from New York.'

'Yes, thank you.' His voice was equally courteous, but there were lines of impatience etched around the straight mouth. Being kept waiting for fifteen minutes had doubtless been a novel experience for the chairman of Mereton Holdings and one he had evidently not enjoyed. But neither had she particularly enjoyed receiving the curt message from his London office yesterday afternoon, informing her that Luke Duncan was already en route to England and would arrive at Rakers' Moon at ten o'clock the following morning. Apparantly Luke Duncan hadn't thought it necessary to ascertain whether the time or the location were convenient for her.

'Did you drive down from London this morning?' Mike enquired casually, her light tone betraying nothing more than polite interest. She had been surprised that he had elected to drive down to Dorset himself, having assumed that a man in his position would have been collected from Heathrow by a chauffeur-driven limousine.

'Last night. I checked in at the Smuggler's Rest.'

Her eyes searched his face quickly. His expression hadn't altered; his terse voice merely reflected his increasing impatience with what he obviously regarded as time-wasting small talk. Her suspicions were confirmed. He still hadn't recognised her!

She lowered her eyes so that he wouldn't see the sparkle of wry amusement. It was hardly flattering to discover that a man who had kissed you only the night before had managed to erase you completely from his memory by morning! Not, she reminded herself forcefully, that she'd found anything remotely amusing about the incident at the time. She'd been furious and resentful, loathing the feeling of utter helplessness as she'd been trapped by powerful arms, at the mercy of that harsh, punishing mouth. *And now he couldn't even remember her.* Pique battled with the amusement and won. Well, she most certainly wasn't going to remind him of their first encounter. She would dismiss it from her own mind as easily as he had evidently done.

'Would you like a coffee? Or a drink?' she asked equably, her expression bland.

'I should prefer to get straight down to business. I have a heavy schedule ahead of me today.'

Mike arched a fine eyebrow. Was she supposed to feel grateful that he had managed to squeeze her into that schedule rather than letting some lesser mortal from his business empire deal with her?

'You've had over three weeks to consider my offer which I'm sure you'll agree is more than fair. I'll have the necessary papers drawn up tomorrow and——'

'Mr Duncan,' Mike interrupted bluntly, 'I have no intention of selling my holding in Kingston Air.'

Jet-black eyebrows knitted together across his forehead. Grey eyes expressed minor irritation.

'Perhaps I should make it quite clear that I will not, under any circumstances, increase my offer.'

Mike looked at him scornfully. Was that what he genuinely believed? That she was indulging in some sort of game, hoping for an improved offer? Matthew had started the small independent airline nearly two decades ago. To him it hadn't been merely a business venture but his whole life. That he had bequeathed his remaining fifty per cent share in the company to her had been an act of faith. Nothing and no one— certainly not this man—would induce her to part with it.

'Perhaps I should make it equally clear that I will not, under any circumstances, sell my shares.' Deliberately she parodied his own crisp, cold enunciation.

'I see.' The irritation in his eyes had deepened to an emotion that Mike found oddly chilling. Luke Duncan, she registered uneasily, was not a man used to being thwarted. That he was utterly ruthless she had no doubt. No one who had achieved his success at the age of thirty-two in the cut-throat world of high finance could fail to be.

She flicked a glance at the grim face. What on earth, she wondered for the hundredth time, had prompted Matthew to sell half his company to Mereton Holdings shortly before his death? It wasn't as if Kingston Air had been in financial difficulties or needed an injection of capital. It simply didn't make sense. Even more baffling was why a huge conglomerate like Mereton Holdings should be interested in becoming financially involved with the small airline. With a total staff of less than fifty, Kingston Air was hardly British Airways. Mike sighed inwardly. For Mereton Holdings, read Luke Duncan, its major shareholder and all-powerful chairman. He was seldom out of the news these days. Either by accident or design, he seemed to court publicity wherever he went. The quality papers referred admiringly to his business acumen while the tabloids were more interested in promoting a playboy image—Luke Duncan and 'close friend' sharing an intimate candlelit meal in some fashionable Paris restaurant...jetting off to a remote, exotic hideaway. The frequency with which the beautiful, glamorous women in his life changed seemed to suggest that he was as ruthless in his private life as in his business one.

Mike was conscious that he was appraising her with the same degree of unenthusiasm.

'Miss Harrington, I can appreciate that you must feel a certain sentimental attachment to Kingston Air. I'm sure we can renegotiate, come to some arrangement whereby you still retain some small interest in the company.'

His patronising tone flicked her on the raw. 'Mr Duncan, I don't think you quite understand. Not only do I intend to retain all my shares, but I plan to take an active part in operating Kingston Air.'

'And what experience do you have of running an airline—or any other business for that matter, Miss Harrington?' He didn't even attempt to keep the derision from his voice.

'None whatsoever,' Mike answered calmly, casually examining a polished fingernail. She was perfectly aware of her lack of administrative experience but if he thought she was going to be intimidated, openly admit to her own doubts and anxieties, he was doomed for disappointment. 'This isn't an interview. I'm not a prospective employee.' Any moment now he would be asking for references, demanding to see her curriculum vitae. 'I'm your partner,' she reminded him sweetly. 'Equal partner,' she added for good measure.

She saw a muscle clench along the line of his jaw. He surveyed her in stony silence for one long moment and then deliberately turned his head, looking out of the window at the silver Porsche parked in the courtyard. It had been a present from her father for her twenty-third birthday, two months ago. He didn't make any comment but he didn't need to. The disdain in his eyes revealed more than mere words. She knew exactly what he must be thinking. Michaelia

Harrington, born with a silver spoon in her mouth, the over-indulged daughter of wealthy electronics manufacturer Daniel Harrington, who simply by virtue of being his only living blood relative had now inherited her grandfather's considerable estate. For a brief moment the knowledge that Luke Duncan despised her, had judged her on such a superficial acquaintance, rankled. She had the unusual urge to defend herself, to tell him the truth, to remind him of last night. And then she shrugged. She had nothing to prove to this man. She didn't care what he thought of her. She didn't even like him, considered him cold-blooded, humourless and totally devoid of any of the charm he was supposed to possess. His opinion was of no value.

'And how long do you think it'll be before the novelty of trying to play businesswoman of the year wears off?'

Of all the arrogant, smug, condescending... Mike looked at him with large, thoughtful hazel eyes. 'We'll have to see, won't we?' she murmured serenely. Did he think he'd be able to goad her into losing her temper that easily? 'And now are you quite sure you wouldn't like a drink? To toast our new partnership?'

His face was like thunder. 'I hardly think that is a cause for celebration,' he grated.

She could hardly disagree with that, Mike admitted ruefully. Still, she consoled herself, Kingston Air was only a very small, insignificant part of Luke Duncan's vast empire. He had maintained a low profile while Matthew was alive, seeming content that Matthew should continue running Kingston Air as before. She wasn't naïve enough to believe that she would be left as severely alone, but with all the other demands on his time, the amount of travelling he undertook, Luke

Duncan simply wouldn't have the time to become involved with the everyday running of the airline. As long as it continued to operate smoothly and at a profit, she doubted whether she would see a great deal of him in person. They would probably have the occasional meeting when he was in England, converse on the telephone, but unless there were any major problems she would probably liaise indirectly with him through one of Mereton Holdings's executives. Her spirits rose. And why should there be any problems? The airline staff were experienced, loyal and enthusiastic. Some of the older members had been with the company since it had first started operating. Mike felt her confidence flooding back. When it came down to it, Kingston Air virtually ran itself anyway.

'I'd like to visit the airport now.'

It was more like a command than a request, Mike observed, fighting back the temptation to leap to her feet and salute.

'I'll fetch my jacket,' she said easily instead.

She followed him out of the house a few minutes later, slamming the heavy front door shut behind her. She gleaned from the way that he immediately strode towards the red saloon parked on the gravel sweep in front of the house that he automatically assumed that he would drive. It was a minor irritation and not worth making a fuss about, she decided quickly.

He held the car door open for her and then walked around to the driver's side, slipping in beside her. He didn't turn the ignition key immediately but gazed up at the huge, red-bricked house in front of them.

'Are you going to sell it?'

Mike turned her head sharply towards him. 'Rakers' Moon, do you mean?' she said pedantically. 'No.' Was he planning to make her an offer for the house as well? she wondered with a swirl of faint hysteria. The house was far too large for one person, expensive to maintain, cold and draughty in the winter—but the idea of selling it was inconceivable. Her mother had been brought up in this rambling old house. She herself had spent holidays here as a child after her mother's death. And in her adult life she had spent as many weekends down here as possible with Matthew. In the past few months, those weekends hadn't been as frequent as she would have liked—if only she'd known how ill he really was ... Quickly she pushed the painful memories to the back of her mind.

'I'm going to live here,' she said quietly, almost as much to herself as the man by her side.

'You're planning to move down from London permanently?' He raised a dark, sceptical eyebrow.

'Naturally,' she returned coolly. 'I can hardly operate Kingston Air by remote control.' Briefly her eyes encountered the dark, cynical grey ones. He still didn't believe she was serious in her intention, she realised, but was perversely determined to regard her as little more than a spoilt child who had just been given an expensive new toy to play with—a toy of which she would quickly become bored. 'Besides,' she added, 'I happen to want to live at Rakers'.'

'Don't tell me, let me guess.' Mockingly he appraised her carefully made-up face, her varnished nails, the deceptively simple designer dress and jacket with the toning, elegant court shoes. 'You're just a simple, old-fashioned country girl at heart.'

'I have a standing order at Harrods for my green wellies.' She smiled sweetly and turned her head away, staring out of the window as the car began to move smoothly along the daffodil-lined drive, and turned

into the narrow lane at the bottom. To the left
stretched rolling green meadows, dotted with black
and white Friesian cows; in the distance lay the Dorset
coast. On a clear day it was still possible to glimpse
the sea from the attic windows at Rakers' Moon, despite the ever-encroaching building development in the
path.

Over to the right, concealed in a copse of trees, lay
the dew pond from which the name of the house had
originated. In bygone days, smugglers had hidden
their contraband from the Excise Men in that pond,
returning on moonlit nights to rake it out. Usually
Mike enjoyed relating the tale but she felt no com-
punction to do so today.

'If you go left at the end of the lane, then left again
at the crossroads, you'll come to the main road. It's
a short cut. Saves going through the village,' she advised the silent man beside her.

He muttered something incomprehensible under his
breath and followed her instructions.

Mike flicked him a sideways glance as they joined
the dual carriageway and headed towards the small
provincial airport where Kingston Air was based. He
wasn't the most scintillating of conversationalists, she
thought drily. Was he by nature this taciturn and un-
communicative, or was he ignoring her deliberately?
Her eyes brushed over the decisive mouth and the tenacious, square jaw. He was undeniably attractive, she
admitted unwillingly, or would be if he deigned to
smile occasionally and the expression in his eyes
weren't so cynical. Her gaze dropped to the lean hands
resting lightly on the steering-wheel. A sprinkling of
fine hairs covered the tanned wrists visible below the
cuffs of the brilliant white shirt. His fingers were long
and misleadingly sensitive. Sensitivity, she was con-

vinced, was not one of Luke Duncan's dominant traits. Through her father, she had encountered numerous men of his ilk—wealthy, ruthless, influential men whose lives were governed solely by ambition. Had circumstances been different, she doubted whether she would have spared Luke Duncan a second thought. Men like him had no appeal for her. She averted her head dismissively but found it wasn't quite as easy to block him from her mind as she'd imagined.

She couldn't seem to relax. His continuing silence was making her feel uncomfortable and edgy, sensations normally alien to her, and it was with something very akin to relief that she saw the airport entrance approaching.

Leaving the car in the staff car park, they walked across to the passenger terminal, Mike finding that even with her long legs she had difficulty in keeping up with the loping strides of her companion. The glass doors slid open in front of them and, as if on cue, the Tannoy crackled into life.

'Kingston Air,' a female voice began hesitantly. 'This announcement is for—er—passengers travelling on Kingston Air flight . . .' A hysterical giggle echoed around the terminal and the Tannoy went dead.

The expression of grim disapproval on Luke Duncan's face was so predictable that, try as she might, Mike found it impossible to hide her involuntary grin.

'You find that amusing?' the cold voice enquired.

Her eyes darkened with exasperation. No one could accuse him of having an overdeveloped sense of humour.

'Kingston Air isn't going to come to a grinding halt because one member of staff has an attack of nerves on the Tannoy,' she said witheringly. She looked across to the line of check-in desks. A scarlet-faced girl in the blue and cream uniform of Kingston Air was standing self-consciously by the Tannoy. 'She's one of the summer temps,' Mike explained lightly. 'She only started on Monday.'

'And is it your usual policy to place untrained, inexperienced and obviously incompetent staff alone on the check-in desk?'

Mike felt her hackles rising in response to the sardonic voice, her antipathy towards the man with the chilling grey eyes increasing by the second. She longed to retaliate but was uncomfortably aware that his criticism was perfectly justified. Matthew would never have allowed one of the seasonal girls to be left unsupervised on the check-in desk until he had judged them sufficiently capable and confident.

'Of course not,' she finally muttered, frowning. 'I haven't actually been down to the airport much over the last few weeks,' she continued rapidly. 'I've been...' She stopped in mid-sentence, appalled with herself. She sounded like a schoolgirl making excuses for not completing her homework. Why did she feel so defensive? Why did she once again have that urgent desire to justify herself to this arrogant male? She took a step away from him.

'Shall we go through to the offices?' Swiftly, she began to walk around behind the check-in desks towards a door marked with the airline logo, and then paused as the Tannoy was switched on again. This time, to her relief, the announcement advising passengers of an indefinite delay to the departure of the next Alderney service due to adverse weather conditions was completed faultlessly. She flicked a glance over her shoulder. Not even Luke Duncan could hold her responsible for fog in the Channel Islands. Then her heart dropped as she listened to a second announcement. The flight to Dinard would also be late in departing. This time for technical reasons.

She braced herself for some scathing comment but to her surprise Luke Duncan remained silent as he followed her down the carpeted corridor. At the far end lay the crew-room and the reservations and accounts offices, from where Mike could hear the reassuring hum of activity.

She pushed open the door to the left, leading into the operations-room, and nearly walked out again. The air was thick with smoke despite the fact that, in deference to the wishes of the majority of the staff, Matthew had designated all the offices, except the crew-room, as non-smoking areas. Two half-eaten crew meals were discarded on top of a filing cabinet; overflowing ashtrays and dirty coffee-mugs were strewn everywhere, even spilling on to the carpet.

The room was occupied by the duty officer, a fair man in his late twenties, who slouched behind a desk covered in paperwork. His collar was undone, his tie loosened at the neck, the sleeves of his crumpled shirt folded back carelessly on his arms.

'Hello, Mike.' He gave a casual smile and then as he registered the figure looming behind the slim girl his manner and posture altered. His back stiffened, and one hand reached up to straighten his tie. 'Good morning, Mr Duncan.' The smile had vanished. 'I'm sorry about the mess,' he added quickly, 'but it's been chaotic this morning. The Alderney weather's been up and down like a Yo-Yo and now Echo November has developed a tech problem.'

Mike nodded, not trusting herself to speak, knowing just how close she was to losing her temper. She wanted to yell at the fair man, order him to tidy up

both the office and his own dishevelled appearance.
His apology had done nothing to appease her anger.
She'd recognised immediately that it had been directed at Luke Duncan as much as her, the duty officer responding instinctively to the other man's
unmistakable air of authority. That Luke Duncan
could command such instant respect aggravated her
still further. But losing her temper would merely make
her look foolish and neither, she admitted fairly, could
the duty officer be held solely responsible for the state
of the room. It would be far more diplomatic to have
a private word with him later. She frowned. Wasn't
she rather over-reacting to a few dirty coffee-mugs
anyway? Would she have felt quite so angry if Luke
Duncan hadn't been here to witness the disorder?

She shot him a rapid glance. After giving the room
a cursory inspection, he had moved across to the
window and stood gazing out over the airfield.
Puzzled, Mike's eyes rested on the broad shoulders.
Wasn't he going to say anything at all? She'd mentally prepared herself for a barrage of searching questions when they arrived at the airport, and yet, except
for his caustic comment about the check-in girl, he
had kept his own counsel. He was quite deliberately
assuming the role of silent observer, she realised with
growing indignation and disquiet, in order to assess
not merely the airline staff—but her!

'How long's the delay on the Dinard?' She addressed the duty officer more calmly than she felt.

'The engineers estimate that it'll take a couple of
hours to fix Echo November.'

Mike resisted the temptation to call up the engineering section and establish the exact problem with
the aircraft.

'Have you issued the passengers with refreshment vouchers?' She hadn't meant to sound quite so brusque and officious.

'They're being given out with the boarding cards.' She heard the note of resentment in the fair man's voice. 'Excuse me,' he murmured with exaggerated politeness as a telephone began to ring insistently.

At the same moment a disembodied male voice floated over the company radio.

'Sierra Tango to Kingston Air.'

Mike hesitated for a second, realised that the duty officer was still occupied on the telephone, and crossed the office to the radio, but she was too late. A lean brown hand had picked up the transmitter.

'Go ahead, Sierra Tango.' Luke Duncan's deep, assured voice was carried over the airways.

'We'll be with you in five. Aircraft serviceable. Eighteen passengers, including one unaccompanied minor.'

'That's copied OK, Sierra Tango. See you on the deck.'

Mike listened to the familiar jargon, her eyes dark with ill-suppressed irritation as they rested on the harsh, unsmiling face. He'd virtually snatched the transmitter from her hand! Did he think she was completely ineffectual, that she was incapable of even answering the radio correctly?

Frustration gnawing inside her, she watched the twenty-seater Twin Otter aircraft land and taxi down the runway towards the control tower. At least the Glasgow flight was on schedule, she thought ruefully.

Two ground hostesses emerged from the arrivals lounge and sauntered casually across the tarmac to meet the incoming passengers. Neither girl, both long-serving members of staff, was wearing the regulation uniform hat or jacket. What was the matter with everyone today? Mike wondered in complete bewilderment. Why today, of all days, did the normally immaculate staff have to look so scruffy and unprofessional? Her eyebrows drew together. And why were two senior girls meeting a small domestic flight when one would have been perfectly adequate, leaving a young, inexperienced seasonal girl to cope singlehanded with the busy check-in desk? And, for that matter, what was the duty officer doing alone in the operations room?

'Where's Andrew?' she demanded shortly. She should have asked that question the moment she walked into the office. Andrew Simpson, the operations manager, had been Matthew's second-in-command since the airline started, and Mike hadn't had any reservations in leaving Kingston Air in his capable hands during her enforced absence. Until now. For the first time, she felt the stirrings of unease. Andrew should be here in this office, overseeing both the operations and the staff.

'He's in the boardroom.' The duty officer shrugged. 'The meetings are tending to get longer and longer each day,' he added ambiguously, but leaving Mike in no doubt as to his meaning.

Eyes reflecting her incredulity, she reached out for the telephone, her immediate reaction to confirm Andrew's whereabouts and summon him back to the office. Then, for the second time that morning, she hesitated, chewing her lower lip with uncharacteristic indecision, and slowly replaced the receiver. The last thing she wanted to do was confront Andrew in front of Luke Duncan. She was acutely conscious of the dark grey eyes exploring her troubled face and suddenly wished with all her being that Luke Duncan was on the other side of the world ... anywhere but in this room, watching her as if she were a performing animal.

'Would you like to come through to Math ... my office, Mr Duncan?' she said coolly, her voice faltering only slightly.

He aquiesced with a curt nod, the expression on his face far from reassuring as she led him across the corridor and into the small office. The furnishings, although comfortable and of a good quality, were functional rather than ostentatious. Black and white photographs of vintage cars, Matthew's second love, adorned the faded yellow walls. The office was still so redolent of her grandfather that Mike found herself tensing each time she entered it. Deliberately avoiding looking at the photographs, she walked across to a filing cabinet, extracted a folder and placed it on the polished table.

'The passenger figures for last month,' she explained briskly. 'They're up on last year.' She paused. Luke Duncan had made no move to pick up the folder, but remained standing, arms folded imperiously across his broad chest, gazing directly at her with narrowed, ominous eyes.

'The boardroom, Miss Harrington?' he enquired with deceptive softness.

Mike gave up the pretence and sat down on a wooden chair by the table, instantly regretting it as it meant she had to crane her neck to look up at him. Unconsciously her fingers flicked the edge of the folder.

'It's the staff euphemism for the airport social club,' she finally admitted reluctantly. He had suspected as much anyway, she was certain.

'Were you aware that Andrew Simpson patronised it while officially on duty?'

'Of course not,' she muttered unhappily.

'His employment will obviously have to be terminated.'

'What?' Mike jerked her head up, appalled by the total lack of emotion and compassion in the cold, clipped voice. 'You want to fire Andrew? Without even asking for an explanation? We don't even know for certain that he is in the club.'

'The whereabouts of Andrew Simpson at this precise moment is hardly the issue. He is paid a generous salary to run the operational side of Kingston Air and supervise the staff. He is clearly doing neither.'

Mike suddenly felt icily calm. 'Andrew has been with the airline for over twenty years. He's always been efficient and competent. You can't sack him for one lapse.' She almost laughed as the full realisation of her words dawned. Luke Duncan *couldn't* do anything without her consent. Any decision would have to be a joint one. 'I won't even consider firing Andrew,' she stated coolly.

'Your loyalty is touching. It's a shame that neither Andrew nor the rest of the staff appear to feel the same degree of loyalty towards you, Miss Harrington.'

Mike's eyes didn't waver from his face—her expression remained determinedly impassive. She wouldn't give him the satisfaction of knowing just how much those words had hurt. And, worse of all, they were completely true. How could she have been so hopelessly egotistical as to assume that the staff would automatically accord her the same respect, loyalty and affection as they had Matthew? She'd called a staff meeting shortly after his death and explained to the staff that, while she knew she could never emulate her grandfather, she intended to continue running the airline exactly as he would have done. She'd wanted to reassure the staff that their jobs were safe—and she'd probably done the exact opposite. Doubtless they had as little faith in her ability to manage Kingston Air as Luke Duncan patently did.

'So what action do you propose that we should take against Andrew?'

The quiet, almost conversational voice, the use of the plural, made her instantly suspicious. He wasn't interested in her opinion.

'Or shall we simply ignore the problem? Forget it? Hope it simply resolves itself?'

His eyes taunted her and to her chagrin Mike felt herself flushing. Deep down she had the sneaking suspicion that, left to herself, that was precisely what she would have done.

'I shall talk to Andrew,' she said squarely, with far more confidence than she felt. What on earth would she say to the man who had been her grandfather's close friend and colleague for two decades, whose airline knowledge so greatly exceeded her own? She'd never imagined having to deal with a situation like this. She'd been relying on Andrew for support and advice, had envisaged them working together as a team, with Luke Duncan a shadowy figure in the background.

'Where does that door lead to?'

Rapidly, she collected her troubled thoughts, totally disconcerted by the seemingly inconsequential question. Frowning with puzzlement, she followed his gaze.

'To the old reservations-room. It was too small once the computers were installed. It's just used as storage space now.'

She watched as he strode across the carpet, flung open the interconnecting door and surveyed the assortment of cardboard boxes piled up on the dusty floor of the inner room.

'Would you arrange to have this cleared out and cleaned up as soon as possible?' he ordered over his shoulder.

'I'll get my mop and duster out straight away,' Mike murmured drily. Evidently 'please' was not a word with which Luke Duncan was familiar. 'Am I permitted to know why? Or do you simply have an obsession about cleanliness?'

He turned round, filling the doorway. 'I'll have the necessary furniture sent down from London,' he continued as if she hadn't spoken.

Mike stared at him blankly for a moment and then comprehension dawned. 'You're planning to come down to the airport full-time? To use that room as your office?' Oh, God, no. She couldn't stand it. She'd be under constant surveillance.

'First prize, Miss Harrington.' He glanced at his wristwatch and moved back across the office to the outer door. 'And now I have business in London to attend to. Good day.'

'But when . . .? Mr Duncan!' Mike rose to her feet in protest and then slumped back weakly in her chair as she heard the sound of brisk, purposeful footsteps retreating down the corridor. Never in her life had she encountered such an infuriating, impossibly rude, exasperating man. How dared he simply walk out on her like that? When exactly did he intend taking up his position at the airport? He hadn't even checked to see if she wanted a lift back to Rakers', she remembered, aggrieved. She leant back in her chair and surveyed the heavy glass paperweight on the desk.

How immensely satisfying it would be to pick that up and hurl it against the wall with all her strength. And how utterly childish. Slowly and unwillingly she began to grin. The morning had been like something from a television farce. Everything that could conceivably go wrong had in fact done so, even down to Andrew's inexplicable behaviour. Was it any wonder that Luke Duncan had decided that he had no option other than to take a more active role in protecting his business interest?

Wryly, she recalled her earlier naïve and optimistic assumption that Kingston Air virtually ran itself. Clearly nothing could be further from the truth. Like any other business, to succeed it required strong, experienced leadership which at present she was unqualified to provide. Whether she liked it or not, as much as she loathed having to admit it, right now Kingston Air needed Luke Duncan at its helm.

She rose to her feet and walked across to survey the adjoining room. It was going to take more than a few pieces of furniture to transfer this room into the kind of luxurious, prestigious office that Luke Duncan must be accustomed to. He was doubtlessly used to having an army of secretaries scurrying around after him. Kingston Air boasted one middle-aged woman who came into the office three times a week. She sighed. How long was he proposing to stay at the airport—surely, with all his other commitments, it must only be a temporary measure? Until he had deemed her competent enough to be left on her own? Or until he had made life so unbearable for her that she gave in and sold out?

She walked across to the window and ran a finger over the dusty sill. Somehow she was going to have to overcome her aversion to him and establish at least some semblance of a working relationship. It would be an impossible situation and detrimental to Kingston Air if they were to be at constant loggerheads, continually sniping at each other.

To be honest, she admitted, she'd been predisposed to dislike Luke Duncan before she'd even met him, influenced by articles she'd read about him in the Press, picturing him as a hard-headed womaniser. But she hadn't expected her reaction to him to be quite so strong. Neither was her preconceived idea of him completely accurate. She'd envisaged that he'd at least try and conceal his tough cynicism beneath a veneer of sophistication and superficial charm. She'd been prepared for him to try and smooth talk her into selling her shares, try and soft soap her with insincere flattery. Yet instead he had been blunt, abrasive and downright offensive. It was that combination of raw, aggressive maleness and arrogant confidence that antagonised her so much, and had sparked off something inside her the moment that she'd laid eyes on him . . . last night.

The moon had been obscured by a blanket of dark cloud as she'd driven along the deserted road, rain lashing against the windscreen. She'd been late leaving London and her thoughts were beginning to stray longingly to the hot meal and comfortable bed that awaited her arrival at Rakers' Moon. She was glad she'd remembered to call John and tell him of her change in plans, a change that had been necessitated by the impending arrival of Luke Duncan the following morning. How much easier it would have been to meet him in London, she thought irritably, and save herself this long arduous journey at night. But by the time she'd received the curt message on her answerphone it had been too late to contact Luke Duncan's London office and rearrange the venue. Part of her had been tempted to simply ignore the message, but then that would just be postponing the inevitable confrontation.

She sighed, disgruntled, and then frowned, instantly alert as she saw the car drawn up on the verge ahead. She touched her brakes lightly. What a filthy night for anyone to break down, she thought with a rush of sympathy, torn between the instinctive desire to stop and help, and the dictates of caution which urged her to drive on. Compromising, she pulled up, but kept the engine revving, prepared to draw away instantly should the need arise.

A tall figure emerged from the shadows, and was clearly illuminated in the bright glare of her headlights. Mike's eyes widened in disbelief. Perhaps if she hadn't been thinking about him, hadn't seen a photograph of him in the newspaper only that morning, she might not have recognised Luke Duncan so instantly, but there was no mistaking the grim, craggy face.

Reassured, she wound down her window. 'Do you have a problem?'

'Of all the damn stupid questions,' a deep voice growled back at her. 'No, I've stopped to admire the view.'

Mike compressed her lips together. She'd just been about to introduce herself, offer him a lift—but she rapidly changed her mind on both accounts. She could appreciate that in the given circumstances he might not be in the best of moods, but to vent his ill humour on her when she'd only been intending to assist him was unpardonably rude. For two pins she'd leave him stranded in the pouring rain on this secluded stretch of road.

'I'll have a look at the car,' she said shortly, relenting, and reached over the back seat for her waterproof coat and flashlight.

'Perhaps it would be more to the point if you'd stop at the next phone box and call out a breakdown service?' he suggested caustically as she scrambled out of the car and pulled the enveloping hood of her huge waterproof coat over her head.

How typically and arrogantly male to assume that simply because she was a female her knowledge of anything mechanical was virtually non-existent, Mike thought scornfully as, ignoring him, she walked around to the boot of her car and opened it. She unfastened the lid of the large metal tool-box, and played the light over its contents, deftly extracting a selection of spanners.

'I take it that those aren't merely accessories but you actually know how to use them,' a voice drawled by her shoulder.

Mike spun round. 'Is there any reason why I shouldn't?' she demanded.

'Oh, God, not a women's libber,' he groaned under his breath as she marched purposefully over to the second stationary vehicle.

She looked at him contemptuously. 'Would you open the bonnet? The release catch is on the right-hand side, just under the dashboard,' she added sweetly.

'I think, even as a mere male, I might be able to manage that,' he murmured drily. 'Would you like me to hold the light for you as well?' he added helpfully as he returned to her side.

Mike handed it to him in silence, bent her head over the open bonnet and inspected the engine. She'd been tinkering with cars since she was ten, helping Matthew renovate his cherished vintage cars during her school holidays.

She located the problem immediately and set to work with a spanner.

'There, that should do it,' she announced, wiping her hands on a rag she'd discovered in her pocket.

'Thank you. Anything serious?'

Mike frowned. It was too dark to see the expression on Luke Duncan's face, but there was something in the deceptively solemn voice that she mistrusted. He was laughing at her, she was certain of it, although why he should find her in the least bit amusing, she couldn't begin to comprehend. Unless...

'The battery terminal was loose,' she explained shortly, rather wishing it had been something far more technical.

'Ah, I see.'

Mike's eyes narrowed, her suspicions increasing. 'You knew exactly what was wrong, didn't you?' she demanded. 'And you just stood there, watching me——'

'Hire cars don't come equipped with either a tool kit or torch,' he cut in. 'Besides,' he added thoughtfully, 'I've never been rescued by a damsel in shining armour before.'

Mike's mouth curled, unamused. 'You being the *chivalrous*, *gallant* knight in distress?' she asked scornfully, still smarting from the fact that she had been hoodwinked so easily. 'That's the last time——'

'You're ever foolhardy enough to stop on a deserted road to help a total stranger.' There was an ominous note in the deep, gravelly voice.

'I knew exactly—ouch!' Mike yelped in protest as his hand snaked around her wrist and he drew her effortlessly towards him. 'Let me——' Her words were drowned as the hard mouth descended on hers, bruising her lips, crushing them mercilessly against her teeth. Frantically, she tried to escape the on-slaught, but she was immobilised by the powerful arms. There was no warmth or gentleness in that harsh, punishing mouth violating her senses. Luke Duncan was simply making a point, illustrating just how vulnerable she was by virtue of being so much physically the weaker.

'You absolute bastard,' she spat out the second he released her and, with tears of fury pricking her eyelids, stormed towards her car.

CHAPTER TWO

MIKE'S eyes darkened, all the resentment and anger she'd experienced the night before tearing back through her. Except that now the anger wasn't directed just at Luke Duncan but also at herself.

She hadn't particularly enjoyed being treated like a reckless idiot, and perhaps her feminine pride had been marginally wounded that Luke Duncan had failed to recognise her this morning, but those were minor irritations. No, what really rankled was the humiliating knowledge that, just for one brief moment when Luke Duncan had held her in his arms last night, she hadn't been fighting her captor but herself, fighting to deny the upsurge of alien sensations that scorched through her, spreading from her swollen mouth to every inch of her being. Her mind had been repelled by his touch but her traitorous body had responded to it.

Mike's eyebrows knitted together in a fierce scowl. She was usually so calm and level-headed, confident of her ability to handle any situation in which she found herself. Yet last night, for the first time in her life, she'd been close to panic. And it was that disturbing revelation that gnawed deep inside her.

She jolted, appalled to discover that subconsciously she'd started to scrawl Luke Duncan's name in the dust on the window-sill. With an abrupt, jerky movement, she swept her hand along the sill, wishing fervently that it was equally simple to erase the man himself from her life. And why was she standing here

31

daydreaming anyway when she had far more urgent
matters to attend to? Like Andrew Simpson, she reminded herself with a heavy heart.

It had been an utterly appalling day, Mike summed
up dispiritedly as she inched the Porsche through the
congested London traffic. She felt jaded, drained both
mentally and physically, and the last thing she felt like
doing this evening was acting as hostess at her father's
dinner party.

Some twenty frustrating minutes later she reached
her destination and swung the Porsche through two
wrought-iron gates, drawing up in front of an im-
posing Edwardian house overlooking Hampstead
Heath. She walked around to the back and entered
by a side-door leading into the kitchen, telling herself
that she ought to check that the preparations for the
evening were well under way, but knowing she was
trying to avoid her father. She simply couldn't face
another argument just now.

'Of course everything's under control,' the stout,
red-faced cook assured her indignantly.

'Those look terrific.' Mike admired a tray of
savouries.

'Here you are.' Her ruffled feathers soothed by the
compliment, the cook benevolently stacked a plate
with the delicacies and handed it to Mike. 'Now don't
you go spoiling your dinner,' she added severely.

'No,' Mike said obediently, hiding her grin. Cook
had been one of the few constant factors in her life,
had outlasted her four stepmothers. And still managed
to make her feel like a recalcitrant six-year-old.

'And now you go on upstairs and get changed.'

Mike nodded, her mouth full. She hadn't realised how hungry she was until now, but then she hadn't eaten since breakfast, she remembered.

'I don't know how you do it. You eat like a horse and there's not an ounce of fat on you.' The cook sighed, glancing mournfully at her own ample proportions, and then looked up sharply. 'Last day tomorrow, isn't it?'

'Mmm,' Mike agreed, edging towards the door.

'Good job, too, if you want my opinion. I never did hold with all that nonsense. Getting up at the crack of dawn, out all night. Coming home looking like something the cat's dragged in. It's just not ladylike. No wonder your father...'

Mike reached the door and, with a quick grin over her shoulder, darted thankfully into the hall. She debated whether to inspect the dining-room, decided it was unnecessary, and bounded up the back stairs to her private suite of rooms. She entered her sitting-room and tossed her jacket over a chair.

'Mike?'

'Come on in, Christina,' she invited in response to the light tap at the door and smiled affectionately as her half-sister glided into the room, wafting expensive perfume with her.

'What do you think? Of the dress?' The eighteen-year-old pirouetted slowly, the rose-coloured chiffon gown swirling gracefully around her.

'You look stunning,' Mike obliged, 'but then you always do.' There was little family resemblance between the two girls. Christina, with her huge black eyes and dark shoulder-length hair, had inherited her sultry beauty from her Italian mother.

Mike moved into her bedroom, inspected her wardrobe without much interest, and selected a sapphire-blue silk dress. She would leave most of these expensive, elaborate dresses when she moved down to Rakers', she decided. She somehow doubted whether she was going to have the time or the inclination for a social life in the next few months. She slipped off her clothes, wrapped a white towelling robe around her, and wandered back into the sitting-room.

'Where is everyone?' She'd been aware of the unnatural peace the moment she entered the house.

'The twins are staying the night with their mother, Tim's gone swimming with a school friend and Olly's in bed,' Christina explained. 'That is, Olly was in bed,' she added as a small tousle-haired boy came bursting through the door and rushed across to Mike with a whoop of delight. He flung his arms around her knees and then spied the plate of tempting savouries.

'For me?' he enquired with beguiling blue eyes.

'You can have two,' Mike relented and the child squatted down on the carpet with his spoils, munching contentedly.

'You spoil him,' Christina observed, swallowing a tiny vol-au-vent and reaching out for a canapé.

'Probably.' Mike smiled vaguely. She felt absurdly protective about the four-year-old and it was him she was going to miss more than anyone when she moved to Rakers'. At least Christina, Timothy and the twins all saw their respective mothers on a regular basis, but Oliver's mother had shown no interest in her son since abandoning him at eighteen months. It constantly puzzled Mike that her father should not only have gained but wanted custody of all his children. In less charitable moments she decided that it was because, with a house full, he was always assured of an audience.

'Come on, poppet.' Mike lifted up her half-brother and kissed his rosy, soft cheek. 'You'll have to clean your teeth again before you go to bed.'

She returned from the nursery a few moments later, slightly irritated to discover Christina sitting in her bedroom, experimenting with a lipstick.

'You'd better hurry up, Mike, or the guests will be arriving,' she murmured, studying her reflection in the mirror.

Mike forbore to mention that if it hadn't been for the interruptions she might well have been ready by now.

Christina suddenly swivelled around on the velvet stool, her pretty face petulant. 'I'll never understand why Daddy always asks you to come to his parties. You really hate them and I'd——'

'Be a much better hostess. I know,' Mike finished with an unoffended grin.

'Well, I'll be nineteen soon,' Christina pouted. 'But then you've always been Daddy's favourite.' The words were said without rancour.

'That's not true,' Mike denied uncomfortably. 'He loves us all, you know that, Chrissy.'

'But you most of all. Even though you never seem to stop arguing with him.' She paused and added with slight malice, 'He's furious with you for not selling your grandfather's shares. And for planning to move down to that awful house in the middle of nowhere. I heard him talking to Luke about it in the library.'

'Luke?' Mike enquired stiffly.

'Mmm. Luke Duncan.' Christina rose to her feet, her eyes glazing over. 'Oh, Mike, isn't he gorgeous?'

'You mean Luke Duncan's actually been to this house?'

Christina frowned. She'd never seen her half-sister look so agitated before. She was always so relaxed and unruffled.

'He's here now,' she explained uncertainly. 'Daddy met him this afternoon at some business lunch or other and asked him to stay with us while he was in London. Mike, are you all right?'

'Of course. Just a bit surprised, that's all,' Mike said quickly, her mind whirling in small, erratic circles. It wasn't as great a coincidence as it seemed that Luke Duncan and her father should have met, she decided, trying to be rational. In fact, considering they inhabited the same jet-setting business world, it was far more surprising that they hadn't encountered each other until now. Neither was it unusual for her flamboyant, gregarious father to invite someone to be a house guest after the briefest of acquaintance. But he had no earthly right to discuss her with Luke Duncan. Or had it been the latter who had instigated the conversation, perhaps suffering from the deluded notion that Daniel Harrington might be able to pressurise or influence his daughter into reversing her decision about Kingston Air? Her mouth curved rebelliously. Let the two men, undoubtedly allies by now, discuss her until they were blue in the face. Neither of them could prevent her from pursuing her intended course of action.

'Do you think I'm too young for him?'

She frowned as Christina's voice penetrated through her thoughts. No need to ask to whom she was referring.

'Oh, don't look at me like that, Mike. I can't help it if I'm not like you. There's nothing wrong with liking someone and wanting to get married.'

'No. Daddy does it all the time.'

The two girls exchanged glances and dissolved into laughter, Mike's tension and anger evaporating.

Christina sobered up and asked thoughtfully, 'Do you ever wonder if your mother hadn't died whether she'd still be married to Daddy?'

'Sometimes,' Mike admitted. In which case it was odd to realise that Christina and the others might never have been born. 'But with Daddy's track record it seems unlikely.' She didn't point out that her father had married Christina's mother just four months after being widowed, something Matthew had never been able to forgive him for. 'Oh, no!' She grimaced as the doorbell rang. 'Surely someone isn't here already?'

Christina obligingly looked out of the window. 'Angela.' She pulled a face. 'Probably arrived early on purpose to catch Daddy on his own.'

'Who's she?' Mike asked without much interest.

'Somebody or other's secretary,' Christina said vaguely. 'Daddy brought her over here yesterday evening to meet us.'

'Wife number six,' Mike uttered drily and headed determinedly for the bathroom. Her father had a moral code of sorts, she supposed. He conducted his numerous affairs with reasonable discretion, only ever inviting to his home those women towards whom his intentions might loosely be called honourable. She shook her head incredulously. Surely he wasn't seriously contemplating another marriage? How many more ex-wives could he afford? It really was about time her father found himself a less expensive hobby, she decided cynically.

She didn't have time for the long, leisurely bath she craved, and settled for a quick shower. She'd make sure that Luke Duncan was seated as far away from her as possible at the dinner table tonight. Then, with any luck, except for a cursory greeting, she could avoid him completely. She'd had more than enough of him for one day.

Christina had departed when she emerged from the bathroom and she sat down on the side of her bed and blow-dried her hair, deliberately straightening out the wilful curls. Why *did* she always agree to act as her father's hostess when he was in between wives? She sighed. Probably for the same confusing reasons that she still lived under his roof, still accepted his lavish presents. Because, despite the constant battles that raged between them, she loved him deeply and couldn't bear to hurt him. And because mixed up with that love was the guilty knowledge that she was a disappointment to him, that she hadn't materialised into the daughter he'd envisaged and wanted. Somehow acting as his hostess was a way of making amends for the fact that she had long ago refused to let him dictate how she should live her own life.

She slipped her dress over her head, clipped on two sapphire earrings, added a matching necklace and then carefully applied her make-up. She walked over to the full-length mirror and grinned mockingly at her reflection. Daniel Harrington's sophisticated, poised, assured eldest daughter. The image was flawless. She pushed her feet into her evening shoes and, without much enthusiasm, made her way downstairs to the drawing-room where guests were entertained before dinner.

Her father was standing by the huge marble fireplace, nursing a whisky in his hand, smiling down at a blonde young woman. A large, powerful man who exuded vitality, there was no trace of grey in the flaming red hair.

'Hello, Daddy.' Mike kissed him lightly on the cheek.

'You look beautiful, Michaelia.' His eyes expressed his approval, a truce evidently to be declared for the duration of the evening. 'Have you met Angela?'

He knew perfectly well she hadn't, Mike thought exasperatedly.

'How do you do?' she murmured politely, smiling at the other girl, observing that she didn't look much older than herself. The day would inevitably arrive when she'd have a stepmother younger than herself, she thought wryly.

She glanced round as the door opened and Luke Duncan walked in accompanied by a vivacious Christina. She'd probably waylaid him in the hall, Mike decided with amusement, ignoring the involuntary cramping of her stomach muscles at the sight of the dark man in full evening dress.

'Good evening, Miss Harrington. How delightful to see you again so soon.'

Rats to you, too, Mike thought silently, meeting the dark, taunting grey eyes evenly. 'Mr Duncan,' she murmured coolly, inclining her head graciously. It seemed utterly ridiculous for them to continue to address each other so formally. 'Excuse me,' she added with frigid politeness and moved away to greet the first arrivals as they were shown into the drawing-room.

She was fully occupied for the next twenty minutes with introductions and ensuring that all the guests were supplied with drinks and canapés. Her initial duties completed, she helped herself to a mineral water and surveyed the room, which was beginning to reverberate with bright, brittle voices. How she loathed all this, inwardly despising herself as she mouthed the expected, insincere platitudes to those around her. To the young ambitious men with their carefully selected girlfriends and fiancées, to the other men with chic, bejewelled women on their arms, who had already achieved success and status. But at what cost to their wives and families? Mike pondered.

Her attention fell on a smooth-faced middle-aged man, his arm draped around a curvaceous brunette. She frowned. She'd liked his wife, a sensible, unpretentious woman who had finally decided that she no longer wanted to play second fiddle to a balance sheet and a succession of young mistresses.

Mike glided towards him, smiling sweetly. 'How's Mary?' she enquired innocently. 'And the girls? Susan must be nineteen by now.' About the same age as the young woman by his side.

She felt a brief, transitory satisfaction as she witnessed the discomfort on his face and then shame engulfed her. She watched him move hurriedly away from her, appalled by her childish conduct. Her father would be furious if he ever learned that she'd deliberately contrived to embarrass one of his business associates. What right did she have to judge someone else, anyway? Would she ever learn to control that impulsiveness—an impulsiveness that she nearly always came to regret later on?

'Ever considered applying for the Diplomatic Service?'

She swung round, disconcerted to find Luke Duncan studying her with inscrutable dark eyes. How long had he been standing there eavesdropping? she wondered disdainfully.

'No. Unfortunately I don't possess your innate subtlety and tact,' she murmured icily. She started to move away when someone inadvertently pushed her from behind, and she was propelled forwards. Strong, male fingers closed over her bare arm to steady her.

'Clumsy idiot. Are you all right?'

'Perfectly, Mr Duncan, thank you,' Mike said haughtily. No, she wasn't all right. Her throat felt tight and her legs were shaky. In order to make himself heard over the steadily increasing noise level, he'd bent his head down towards her. The stubborn line of his jaw was on a level with her eyes, the straight, decisive mouth a few inches higher. The scent of expensive male aftershave assailed her senses. Memories of last night curdled and erupted in her head.

'May I have my arm back?' she said lightly, her casual tone giving no indication of that quite illogical upsurge of panic. She felt the pressure of his fingers ease as he relaxed his hold, and, thankfully, she made her escape.

She forced herself to mingle with the other guests, smiling brightly, bluffing with practised ease when she couldn't recall someone's name, dutifully admiring the other women's gowns. She deliberately gave Luke Duncan a wide berth, some sixth sense seeming to alert her to his whereabouts, even when he wasn't in direct vision. At the moment, he was facing her across the room, surrounded by people yet curiously apart from them, present physically, but mentally isolated, an expression of utter world-weariness in his eyes. Mike felt a mounting annoyance. If he was so bored, why had he bothered to accept her father's invitation? He could at least pretend to enjoy himself.

Even more irritating was the fact that his remoteness and air of indifference seemed to send out a direct challenge to virtually every woman in the room to be the one he noticed. In a room full of wealthy, successful, good-looking men, it was he who drew and held female eyes. Usually it was Daniel Harrington who commanded all the attention on such occasions, but tonight he had been well and truly usurped. No wonder Luke Duncan was so impossibly arrogant and self-assured, Mike thought with a viciousness that startled her. He didn't even have to try and be amusing or pleasant—he just stood there, cold and aloof, and women were drawn to him like mindless moths.

She wasn't unduly surprised to find that Christina had managed to seat herself next to him at the dinner table. She herself was at one end of the rectangular table opposite her father and, from her vantage-point, she had a clear view of all the diners.

Christina, she observed with a mixture of exasperation and amusement, was smiling up at Luke Duncan with wide, flirtatious eyes, seemingly determined to gain and keep his attention. As the soup dishes were whisked efficiently away amid murmurs of appreciation, Christina placed a small, soft hand on his arm and murmured something in his ear. Transfixed, Mike watched in disbelief as Luke Duncan threw back his head and laughed. His whole face was transformed, the lines of cynicism erased, his teeth white and even against the tan of his skin, his eyes crinkling at the corners, appearing blue instead of that chilling grey. He was smiling down at Christina now, looking more relaxed than Mike had ever seen him, an expression of amusement etched on his face. How on earth had her half-sister managed to break through that icy reserve? Mike wondered incredulously. She was caught completely off guard as Luke Duncan abruptly turned his head towards her, as if sensing her scrutiny. The smile vanished from his lips. For one imperceptible second, Mike's eyes were locked into his, and as she stared into the deep, dark unfathomable depths she felt an inexplicable *frisson* of unease and foreboding crawl across her skin.

'Thank you very much, sir. Goodnight.'

Mike stood by her father's side on the wide front doorstep, watching as the last of their guests departed. Judging from the lateness of the hour, the evening had been a success.

'Bright young man, that. He'll go a long way.' Daniel Harrington commented as he shut the front door. 'You could do a lot worse than Philip Dawson, Michaelia. I'll invite him over to lunch one Sunday.'

Mike smiled vaguely, too weary to argue, wondering if her father would ever give up parading his idea of eligible, suitable young men before her as if she were at a public auction. If—and it was a very big if—she ever did decide to marry, it would be to someone as far removed as possible from any of the men who had been present here tonight. It would be to a man who respected her as an individual and an equal, to a man who didn't regard marriage as little more than one more strategic career move, the acquisition of yet another asset in the form of a resident hostess and mother of future heirs. Mike shook herself mentally. Why was she thinking about marriage, even in the abstract? The very last thing she wanted to complicate her life at the moment was an involvement of any kind—let alone a husband.

'I'm just going to check everything's all right in the kitchen, and then I'm off to bed,' she murmured. 'Goodnight, Daddy.' She supposed that she ought to have returned to the drawing-room to wish Luke Duncan a courteous goodnight too, she thought a few moments later as, stifling a yawn, she made her way upstairs. Still, she doubted that he would notice the admission.

'Mike, wait for me.'

She paused on the landing as Christina came bounding up the stairs behind her.

'Guess what?' she whispered hoarsely, her face aglow with excitement. 'Luke's asked me to go to a concert with him tomorrow night.'

Mike blinked, pushing her door open. 'A pop concert?' she said doubtfully, fully acquainted with Christina's taste in music, but unable to imagine Luke Duncan attendant at such a venue.

'Course not. It's some orchestra or other. At the Albert Hall.' Christina followed her into the sitting-room.

'But you don't know anything about classical music.' Mike kicked off her shoes with relief.

'I like the *1812 Overture*,' Christina said defensively, 'and...' she searched for inspiration '...that tune Torvil and Dean used to skate to.'

'Ravel's *Bolero*,' Mike put in helpfully, going into her bedroom and starting to remove her make-up with cold cream.

'Mmm.' Christina danced in after her. 'What dress shall I wear? That new black one, I think. And I'll put my hair up, too.' She heaved a dreamy sigh. 'He's so wonderful, those gorgeous eyes... Did you know he's got an apartment in Paris and Geneva as well as New York? And a house in——'

'Chrissy,' Mike cut in, sensing that if she didn't make a firm stand this was going to develop into a long session, and the thought of staying up half the night, hearing Luke Duncan's virtues being extolled, was enough to make her wince. 'I really must get some sleep.'

'The trouble with you, Mike, is that you've become utterly boring. You're not interested in anything but that stupid airline.' Christina flounced from the room and slammed the door shut behind her.

Mike pulled a rueful face, not unduly concerned by the exit, accustomed to Christina's minor tantrums by now. Had she become boring...? So boring that Luke Duncan found her younger half-sister's company infinitely more entertaining than her own? That line of thought was ridiculous. The only interest she wanted Luke Duncan to evince in her was a purely professional one. She frowned. Christina had been right to a degree, though. Kingston Air did occupy a great deal of her thoughts at present. But then she'd always had a tendency to be single-minded, even as a child, throwing herself body and soul into whatever currently occupied her interest. Mechanically she finished her preparations for bed and slipped in between the sheets, switched off the bedside lamp and stared up into the darkness. Wasn't that fundamental characteristic partly the reason why she'd deliberately shied away from any emotional involvements in her life? Because deep down she had the uneasy suspicion that if she ever did fall in love it would be with the same single-mindedness that she did everything else, and the idea of her personal happiness being totally dependent on one man was intolerable?

She turned over and pummelled her pillow into a more comfortable shape, but, tired as she was, sleep perversely continued to elude her. Her mind was too active, retracing the events of the day with depressing clarity. Christina and Luke Duncan...their linked names kept whirling around in her head. She flicked her eyes open again. Luke Duncan was far too old for Christina, not merely in years, but in experience.

Despite her contrived air of sophistication and world-liness, Christina was the product of a strict, single-sex boarding-school and Daniel Harrington's rigid, hypocritical double standards. Her conversation might revolve around men, but her actual experience of them was virtually nil. With her immature, romantic no-tions of love, she would be an easy prey to a man like Luke Duncan. Mike's hands clenched into fists under the bedclothes. If he hurt Christina in any way, she'd... Do what exactly? She started to grin. She didn't normally have this propensity for melodrama! Why did she feel so disturbed and wound up inside? Luke Duncan was only taking Christina to a concert, for goodness' sake. The unwanted image of a pair of dark, unsmiling eyes swept into her head and with great determination she began to think of endless sheep jumping over a five-barred gate.

The insistent peal of the alarm clock summoned Mike to wakefulness as the first rays of dawn filtered into the bedroom. Bleary-eyed, she scrambled out of bed and padded towards the bathroom, emerged a short time later and dressed rapidly in a pair of faded jeans and an old sweatshirt, pulling a pair of dark green overalls over the top. She brushed her dishevelled hair absently, quickly removed the nail polish she'd for-gotten the night before, and crept quietly from the room and down the stairs, careful not to disturb the remainder of the somnolent household.

She could smell the aroma of grilled bacon as she reached the hall and sighed. Despite her repeated as-sertions that she was quite capable of getting her own breakfast when she was on early shift, Cook still in-sisted on rising to prepare it.

She pushed open the door of the small breakfast-room that adjoined the kitchen and faltered at the unexpected sight of the dark-haired figure sitting behind the round table, sipping a cup of tea. What was Luke Duncan doing up at this hour? Mike wondered irritably, never at her best in the morning. She absorbed the black tracksuit he was wearing and her mouth curled disdainfully. He was probably one of those nauseating individuals who ran a couple of marathons before breakfast, rounding it off with a strenuous work-out in the gym. He certainly looked strong and fit enough to do so, she admitted reluctantly, surveying the long, muscular frame.

'Morning,' she grunted, moving into the room.

He turned his head, his gaze moving slowly over the mop of unruly copper curls, the freckled face devoid of all make-up, and rested on the shapeless, ill-fitting overalls that couldn't quite conceal the feminine lines beneath.

'I'm going to work,' Mike said shortly, forestalling any caustic comments on her appearance, refusing to admit to that increasing regret that she hadn't at least applied a touch of lip gloss.

'Really?' He raised a dark eyebrow. 'Dressed like that?'

She looked at him calmly. 'I'm a licensed aircraft engineer.' The knowledge that she'd actually managed to disconcert the powerful, assured Luke Duncan was immensely satisfying. He'd had no idea at all, she realised, glimpsing the astonishment in his eyes. But then why should he? She'd deliberately chosen not to tell him for reasons she couldn't wholly understand, and her father most certainly wouldn't have enlightened him. Daniel Harrington preferred as few people as possible to know that, despite his fierce opposition, his eldest daughter had elected for a career which necessitated spending her working life clad in unflattering overalls with grease and oil all over her hands.

She poured herself a cup of tea and smiled her thanks as Cook appeared with a laden plate and set it before her, conscious all the while of Luke Duncan watching her intently.

'And does your mechanical expertise extend to hire cars?' he enquired conversationally as soon as they were alone again.

Mike swallowed a piece of grilled tomato. So he'd finally put two and two together. 'Hire cars?' she repeated innocently, meeting the grey eyes evenly.

'Damsel in shining armour,' he murmured thoughtfully.

Mike frowned. 'How many letters?' She badly wanted to burst out laughing and it took every ounce of self-discipline to keep her face straight.

'Nine. Begins with M and ends in A.' There was the suspicion of a grin at the corners of the straight mouth, a glint of amusement in the dark eyes, and Mike felt her stomach dip, the sheer force of his attraction gripping her without any warning.

'Give up?' He rose to his feet and moved around the table.

Her breakfast forgotten, Mike's whole attention was concentrated on the figure looming over her. She dared not look directly into his face until she'd regained her composure and instead found her gaze resting on the unsettling expanse of tanned skin, liberally covered with fine dark hairs, revealed at the open neck of his tracksuit.

'Shall I give you a clue?' Stooping, he placed a firm hand under her chin, and slowly and deliberately lowered his head down towards her. Violently, Mike jerked back her chair, recoiling from the touch of that hard, fierce, expert mouth against her own.

'So it was you!' Mocking grey eyes surveyed her flushed, agitated face with ill-disguised satisfaction. 'You weren't driving the Porsche,' he added thoughtfully, moving away from her and returning to his chair.

'No.' How immensely flattering to know that the car would have made a more lasting impression on him than she had done. 'I'd borrowed the Mini from the garage where the Porsche was being serviced.' She didn't want to talk about the subject any longer, didn't even want to think about it. Deliberately she resumed eating her breakfast, feeling as if every mouthful would choke her, but determined that Luke wouldn't suspect just how rattled she felt. When had she started thinking of him by his first name?

'I assume by his silence on the matter that your father isn't too enthralled with the fact that you make a living as a grease monkey?'

Mike flung down her knife and fork, gold flecks sparkling in her hazel eyes as she surveyed the figure leaning back casually in his chair. 'A grease monkey?' she flared. 'It takes longer to train an aircraft engineer than a pilot. I'm hardly a . . .' She stopped as she saw the expression on his face. He had quite deliberately been trying to provoke her—and he had succeeded, she admitted with a reluctant grin. 'No, he isn't,' she murmured, answering his question. Why had she never noticed before just how sensuous was the line of that firmly chiselled mouth? And why did that thought have to occur to her now of all times?

'And his opposition made you ever more determined to go ahead with it?' He quirked a dark eyebrow at her.

She was disconcerted by his astuteness. 'Partly,' she admitted. She had served her long apprenticeship with a major airline at Heathrow and there had been numerous times, particularly during the first arduous year, when she'd been tempted to chuck it all in, but pride had kept her going, the thought of having to admit failure, not just to her father but also to Matthew, the only person who had ever supported and encouraged her, inconceivable.

'And now you've decided to be equally stubborn about Kingston Air?'

Mike raised her head and gazed at him serenely. She wasn't going to bite this time.

'Why don't you just give up?' If she was stubborn, she had met her match in this man, she thought wryly. 'I made my decision a month ago when I handed in my notice at work. I'm hardly going to change my mind at this stage. So why don't you simply accept that you'll never have complete control of the airline?'

He leant back even further in his chair, linked his hands behind his dark head and surveyed her with narrowed eyes.

'Of course there is one option left. I could always ask you to marry me.'

CHAPTER THREE

'You could,' Mike agreed evenly, placing her knife and fork together on her plate.

'Imagine the damage to my male ego if you rejected me though,' Luke continued gravely.

'Doesn't bear thinking about,' she retorted drily, desperately trying not to burst into laughter. The idea of anyone or anything managing to even superficially scratch—let alone dent—Luke Duncan's ego was ludicrous. As ludicrous as this present conversation. 'I gather you're fully acquainted with the terms of my grandfather's will.'

'In the event of your marriage, half your shares in Kingston Air are to be transferred to your husband,' he summarised succinctly and frowned thoughtfully. 'I wonder what prompted Matthew to add such an extraordinary codicil.'

'He must have had his reasons,' Mike said absently. She had already discussed this topic at length with Christina and had no wish to do so with Luke Duncan. 'More tea?' she enquired in an attempt to change the subject.

'Thanks.' He pushed his empty cup towards her. 'Presumably he was hoping to ensure that you took marriage a little more seriously than your father.'

Mike slammed down the teapot. She had already reached that conclusion herself, but, although she might have deep reservations about her father's casual attitude to matrimony, she wouldn't tolerate any criticism of him from an outsider. 'You know exactly nothing about——'

'Don't get on your high horse,' Luke cut in before she was fully launched on her defensive tirade. 'How your father conducts his life is of no concern to me. I was merely suggesting that Matthew might have preferred that you didn't emulate him.'

His remark did nothing to appease her. 'At least my father only breaks up his own marriages and not other people's,' she muttered.

'And what is that supposed to mean?'

'Come on, now,' she said witheringly, 'your relationship with Lisa Sinclair—*Mrs* Lisa Sinclair hasn't exactly been discreet.'

She wanted to make him angry, put him on the defensive, and felt deflated when he simply took a sip of tea and then studied her with an expression of complete unconcern.

'Are you an avid reader of the gutter Press?' he asked conversationally.

Mike flushed. It was only recently that she'd started to flick through the more sensational of the tabloids strewn about at work, fired with curiosity to read anything she could about her new partner. The photograph of Luke and the beautiful English star of a popular, successful American soap opera, together with a suitably ambiguous caption, had appeared last week.

'Disappointed that I'm not going to deny the charges—or would you prefer that I confessed all so that you could have your own personal exclusive?'

'I'm not interested in the details of your sordid private life,' she bit back and leapt to her feet. It was impossible to have even the rudiments of a rational, normal conversation with this man. 'I'm going to work,' she informed him shortly and headed for the door.

'Incidentally, did you speak to Andrew Simpson yesterday?'

She paused. 'Yes, I did,' she murmured vaguely without turning round.

'And?'

Sighing, she looked at him over her shoulder. 'He told me that one of the local travel agents had turned up unexpectedly at the airport and he'd taken him over to the club for an early lunch.'

'Really?' He raised a cynical eyebrow. 'And you believed him?'

Of course she hadn't believed him! But she'd been weak enough to pretend to, she reminded herself unhappily. 'What did you expect me to do?' she flared. 'Call him a liar to his face?' Why couldn't Luke appreciate just how difficult she found it to deal objectively with Andrew Simpson?

He shook his head slowly, regarding her as if she were a wayward child. 'You may know one end of an aircraft from another but you have a great deal to learn about staff management.'

Mike slammed the door shut behind her. She couldn't have stayed and listened to that smug, patronising chauvinist one moment longer.

Why couldn't Luke Duncan have been a different sort of man? she wondered dejectedly a few moments later as she drove the Porsche out of the front gates. Someone patient and understanding, who didn't regard her inexperience simply as a subject for his scorn and derision?

The traffic was light at this hour of the day and she headed along the near empty road towards Heathrow. Her last day at work. Perhaps the last time she'd ever be a practising engineer. A wave of deep sadness engulfed her.

'I'm going to miss you all so much.' Mike dashed away the tears from her eyes. Oh, heavens, she was becoming sentimental and maudlin. Slowly her eyes moved around the small, packed office, absorbing each familiar face with affection. These men had formed an integral part of her life for the past six years and it was going to be an even greater wrench to leave them than she'd imagined.

'Just when we've finally taught you to make a decent brew-up, you're going,' someone quipped.

Mike grinned. No one had ever allowed her to forget her first day here. Accustomed to being waited on hand and foot all her young life, she'd been indignant to discover that her new duties included fetching and carrying, and making seemingly endless mugs of tea.

'I've come here to train as an engineer,' she'd informed the chief engineer haughtily, 'not to be a skivvy and general dogsbody.'

'You've come here to do as you're damn well told. Like it or get out,' had been the brusque, unsympathetic reply.

'I was a real spoilt brat in those days, wasn't I?' Mike observed to no one in particular. It had taken her a long time to adjust to these outspoken, down-to-earth men and even longer to earn their respect and liking. They, in turn, had found it difficult to accept a girl into their all-male preserve.

'Here, Mike, have a top-up.'

She tried to refuse, but her protests were ignored and her glass replenished.

She had been deeply touched that every single one of her colleagues had turned up for the informal farewell party that had started after her early shift had ended. Even those now on duty had made brief appearances to wish her well, toasting her rather reluctantly with soft drinks.

Mike rubbed a hand over her eyes. She was beginning to wish that she'd stuck to orange juice herself. She rarely drank alcohol, not much liking the taste, but it would have been churlish to refuse the champagne that had been produced in her honour. She took a sip from her glass. The bubbles seemed to be going straight to her head. She was beginning to feel distinctly dizzy and hot. One thing was certain, she was in no fit state to drive home and her original plan to go down to Rakers' this evening would have to be postponed until tomorrow. All she really felt like doing was falling asleep. She'd have to arrange for a taxi to collect her soon, or, better still, ask Christina if she would come over to the airport in one and drive them both home in the Porsche. That way she'd have her car ready for the morning.

'Bye, Mike. Got to go, I'm afraid. Duty calls.' A huge man dressed in overalls picked her up in a bearhug. 'Take care, kiddo,' he murmured as he set her back on her feet, and rumpled her red curls. 'And good luck.'

She kissed him on the cheek amid approving cheers and then inched her way across the congested room to the telephone. It was difficult to hear properly because of all the noise in the background, but Oliver's nanny, who answered the call, assured Mike that she'd pass on the message to Christina.

'Mike, heard this one?'

Grinning, she perched herself on the ledge of the office table, swinging her jeans-clad legs, and listened to the joke of which she inevitably was the good-natured butt. It was once everyone had started teasing her unmercifully that Mike had realised that she'd finally been accepted into their masculine midst.

The party began to break up slowly and she flicked a glance at her wristwatch. Christina should be here by now. She frowned. Surely her half-sister wasn't still in a huff about last night . . .?

'Someone here for you, Mike.' A security officer beckoned to her from the open office door.

Her eyebrows knitted together as she focused her eyes on the familiar figure looming by the side of the uniformed man. Slowly, she scrambled down from the table, astounded to discover how wobbly were her legs. With great deliberation, she walked carefully across the room.

'What are you doing here?' She looked up at Luke Duncan unenthusiastically.

'Christina wasn't able to come,' he informed her.

'So you came to fetch me instead? How kind of you to go to so much trouble.' She winced inwardly as she saw his mouth tighten. She hadn't meant to sound so sarcastic and ungracious. This man just seemed to bring out the worst in her. It had been kind of him, if surprising, to stand in for Christina. Why couldn't she have simply thanked him naturally as she would anyone else? Unconsciously she pressed a hand to her temples. Her head was beginning to ache dreadfully.

'Have one for the road?' A young engineer proffered a glass.

'I think she's had quite sufficient,' Mike heard a cool voice answer for her. How cold and grim Luke looked, she mused. Hardly the life and soul of the party. She felt his hand on her arm.

'Time we were going.'

'But I haven't said goodbye to everyone yet,' Mike wailed.

'I'll give you a lift over to the car park in my van,' the security officer offered.

'No, thanks all the same. The fresh air will do her good.'

Mike scowled. *Her?* Did Luke have to keep talking about her as if she weren't present? Couldn't he remember her name?

'You're hurting me,' she complained bitterly as she was frog-marched along the corridor. She winced as they emerged into the afternoon sunshine and would have stumbled if the hand around her arm hadn't tightened. Her legs felt as if they were about to give way beneath her and it seemed to take every ounce of concentration to keep placing one foot in front of another.

'Keys?' Luke demanded as they finally reached the car park, and Mike fumbled in her pocket to retrieve them. He unlocked the passenger door of the Porsche and unceremoniously bundled her in.

She slumped back in the seat as he turned on the ignition. Her throbbing head felt as if it were on fire and yet she couldn't seem to stop shivering. She wanted to sit up straight but it seemed to require too much effort to do so. The movement of the car was beginning to make her feel nauseous.

'I don't feel too good,' she muttered through dry lips. 'P-please stop the car,' she begged desperately. Her head was spinning round and round in circles. Perhaps if she just closed her eyes for a second...

The car had stopped. They must have arrived home, Mike thought vaguely. Slowly she opened her heavy eyelids and frowned, totally disorientated as she stared up at the white ceiling. She was lying in a huge double bed and it was almost dark, the last rays of sun filtering into the room. A room that most definitely was not her own, and one in which she'd never in her life been before.

Weakly, Mike manoeuvred herself into a sitting position and surveyed her surroundings. The only familiar objects were the blue sweatshirt and denims folded neatly over a wicker chair beside a dressing-table, the top of which was covered with an array of expensive cosmetics. Briefly her eyes rested on the silk négligé hung up on the door. Where was she? she wondered with growing agitation. And where was Luke? If only her head didn't feel so muzzy and she could think clearly.

She flung back the duvet and padded across the thick white carpet to retrieve her clothes. Even the simple task of pulling on her jeans and sweatshirt seemed to take all her energy.

She glimpsed her reflection in the dressing-table mirror and grimaced. The freckles stood out violently against her pallid skin and her eyes were dull and listless. She raked a hand through her dishevelled hair but the curls just bounced back in an unruly mop over her head.

Slipping on her shoes, she opened the bedroom door and discovered a small, square carpeted hall. Selecting a door at random, she pushed it open.

Luke was sprawled in a chintz-covered armchair, long legs stretched out in front of him, reading a book. He had removed his jacket, loosened his tie and looked completely at home.

'You look terrible,' he greeted Mike casually, lifting his head to study her slight figure.

'I've always found it difficult to deal with extravagant compliments,' she muttered sourly. She felt even worse than she looked, if that were possible. 'Where am I?' It was odd how reassuring was the sight of Luke, the momentary alarm she'd experienced earlier instantly dismissed.

'About ten miles from Heathrow.'

That wasn't what she meant and he knew it. He was deliberately being aggravating, she thought tetchily. 'Who does this flat belong to?' she snapped back.

'Friend of mine,' he returned laconically.

'I see.' Her lips compressed together, recalling the feminine contents of the bedroom. 'And what exactly am I doing in your *friend*'s flat?' she enquired coolly.

'You were sick,' he said bluntly.

'Oh, no.' Mike slumped down into an armchair. She'd never felt so humiliated in all her life. 'In the car?' she asked in a small voice.

'I managed to stop in time and throw you into a convenient ditch.'

'Thanks a lot,' she muttered.

'But not particularly craving a repeat performance,' he continued calmly, 'I decided it might be advisable to stop as soon as possible and let you sober up. This happened to be the nearest, most obvious place.' He surveyed her ashen face thoughtfully. 'Don't you remember anything?'

'I'm beginning to,' she mumbled, as vague, fragmented memories floated into her head, confirming the veracity of his words. 'I wasn't drunk, though,' she denied.

'You gave a pretty good imitation of it,' he commented drily.

'But I only had two glasses of champagne,' she protested vehemently. Surely not enough to warrant this splitting headache? And she still felt so weak and queasy.

He shrugged. 'Did you have any lunch?'

'Not much,' she admitted. She chewed her lip, studying Luke with puzzled eyes. She would have expected him to relish this situation, to be making cheap, caustic jibes at her expense, and yet he was treating it all so matter-of-factly.

A sudden, uncomfortable thought struck her. 'I—er—suppose I put myself to bed,' she murmured with studied casualness, remembering that she'd only been clad in her bra and pants on waking.

'You were *non compos mentis*, sweetheart, out for the count, in no fit condition to do anything.'

'So who——?' Heated colour suffused her pale cheeks at the thought of Luke performing the intimate task.

'I put you to bed,' a firm female voice intervened. 'Don't let him tease you.'

Mike turned her head, her eyes widening at the sight of the beautiful, fair-haired woman standing in the doorway, holding a tray of coffee.

'I was just about to bring this to you.' Smiling, she handed Mike a mug.

'Thank you.' There was something so familiar about the blonde woman with the startling, vivid blue eyes and yet she was certain she'd never met her before.

'Michaelia Harrington—Lisa Sinclair.' Luke drawled the introductions from his chair.

Mike stiffened immediately. She didn't believe it. How could Luke have had the audacity to bring her to his mistress's flat? Her eyes darkened with revulsion. She'd actually been asleep in their bed!

'Michaelia thinks that you and I are in the throes of a torrid, passionate affair, Lissy. In fact,' Luke continued thoughtfully, 'she probably thinks that this is our cosy little love-nest.'

Mike almost dropped her mug of coffee. Furiously, she glared at her tormentor. How could he be so crass and insensitive, deliberately set out to embarrass her like this?

'Do you really think that?' Lisa Sinclair's mouth curved with amusement. 'You've not been reading all that trash in the papers, have you?'

'No, of course not.' Mike tried desperately to sound nonchalant, conscious of a pair of dark grey, taunting eyes resting on her crimson face. She rarely blushed and now she'd done so twice in as many minutes.

'Luke and I are cousins, actually,' the fair woman murmured, sinking elegantly on to the sofa. 'And I'm married to his best friend.' She pulled a wry face. 'Two basic facts that the Press tend to conveniently forget.'

Mike gave a sickly smile.

'I had to go over to New York to do some promotion work last week and, as I absolutely loathe staying in hotels, Luke put me up in his apartment.' She grinned. 'The gossip-mongers had a field day with that.'

'Don't you mind?' Mike asked, bewildered by the other woman's apparent unconcern. 'Couldn't you sue or something?'

'If I started a lawsuit every time a newspaper printed an inaccuracy about me, I'd spend my entire life in the court-house.' She shrugged. 'Besides, it's all free publicity. And no one with any sense genuinely believes all the rubbish they read, do they?'

'No,' Mike mumbled, not daring to look at Luke. Feeling thoroughly squashed and chastened, she finished off her coffee in silence.

'Hope to see you again.' Lisa smiled as Mike thanked her awkwardly for her hospitality. 'Luke, now you're going to be in England for a while, you must come down to the Cotswolds and see us. Tom and I have just bought this gorgeous old cottage down there,' she explained to Mike. 'Make sure Luke brings you with him when he comes.'

Mike smiled vaguely, wondering exactly what Lisa thought was her relationship with Luke and then decided that the other girl had merely extended the invitation to her through courtesy on the spur of the moment, and it wasn't to be taken seriously.

'Why didn't you tell me Lisa Sinclair was your cousin?' she turned on Luke the moment they were sitting in the Porsche. 'You deliberately set out to make a fool of me!' Her voice seethed with resentment.

'I didn't make a fool of you,' he contradicted her with infuriating calmness. 'You managed to do that quite successfully all by yourself.' It was difficult to gauge the expression on his face as he turned to look at her. 'You shouldn't jump to conclusions about people,' he said quietly, clicking on his seatbelt.

Mike didn't answer, but digested his words in silence, staring out into the darkness. She wanted to defend herself but had the uncomfortable feeling that he might be justified in his criticism. She frowned uneasily. Did she really leap to conclusions about people without knowing anything about them, judging them simply from first impressions? She stole a glance at the man by her side, the light from a street lamp illuminating the strong, hard profile. She had been determined to dislike Luke from the beginning, determined to think the worst of him. To discover, as she had this afternoon, that he was capable of tolerance, even of kindness, disturbed her for some inexplicable reason. She didn't want to admit that he might have any redeeming qualities, didn't want to find her attitude towards him changing.

Lost in thought as she was, it wasn't until they drew up outside her father's house that Mike's memory was jolted. 'You were supposed to go to a concert with Christina tonight!'

'I telephoned her from Lisa's and explained that I was unavoidably detained,' Luke murmured drily.

'I suppose it's too late for you to go now.' How disappointed Christina was going to be, Mike thought guiltily. And angry, she added with a sinking heart. 'I'm sorry for ruining your evening,' she muttered as Luke held the car door open for her. 'And thank you for...rescuing me this afternoon,' she added reluctantly.

'I guess the scores are about even now.' He quirked an eyebrow at her but she couldn't bring herself to grin back.

The hall was deserted as they entered the house.

'Everyone must be getting dressed for dinner.' The thought of food made Mike feel queasy again. 'I think I'll go straight on up to bed,' she murmured. 'Goodnight.'

He didn't reply, but stood looking down at her in silence. Mike, poised with one foot on the bottom of the stairs, found that she couldn't move any further, her eyes drawn to his face.

Holding her gaze, he bent his head towards her and brushed her lips with his mouth. It was the lightest of kisses and yet it teased every nerve-ending in her body, and sent an uncontrollable sweep of pleasure surging through her.

'Goodnight, Michaelia.

He took a step away from her, his expression unreadable, and then walked purposefully down the hall towards the drawing-room.

With a confused feeling of dissatisfaction, Mike slowly mounted the stairs, totally unaware of the pulse beating erratically at the base of her neck.

'So you're back!' Christina came walking along the landing towards her, her pretty face masked with petulance. 'I suppose Luke is with you?' There was no mistaking the jealousy or the implication in her voice.

'Yes,' Mike said quietly, overwhelmingly glad that her half-sister hadn't witnessed Luke's unexpected—and unwanted, she reminded herself forcefully—kiss a few seconds earlier.

'You really are a hypocrite, Mike. You pretend you don't like Luke and then you——'

'Chrissy, before you start, let's get one thing clear,' Mike cut in wearily. 'I'm not in the least bit interested in Luke. He's not my type. We're business partners, that's all.'

'And that's what you've been doing all afternoon? Discussing business?' Christina's dark eyes flashed angrily. 'I wish I'd come to pick you up myself and skipped my hairdressing appointment. It was all for nothing anyway. Luke's not taking me out now and it's all your fault.'

'I'm sorry, Chrissy.' Mike sighed. What was the use of trying to explain anything to Christina in her present mood? 'I'm going to bed,' she said abruptly and, with horror, felt the bitter rise of nausea in her throat.

*   *   *

The grey-haired doctor murmured something incomprehensible and then relented as he saw his patient's look of bewilderment. 'Gastric flu to the layman,' he translated cheerfully. 'And a particularly nasty bout. Still, you're young and fit. A couple of weeks' rest and you'll be up on your feet again.'

'But I can't lie in bed for two weeks!' Mike gazed at the family practitioner with dismay. 'I'm far too busy.'

'You'll do as you're told for once, my dear. You're a very sick young woman.' He snapped his bag shut. 'Once your temperature's down, I'll allow you up for a couple of hours each day as long as you promise to take things easy. Keep warm, drink plenty of liquids. I'll be back tomorrow to see how you are.'

The moment the doctor departed, Christina burst into the bedroom, her face flushed, clutching a basket of exquisite blooms. 'Aren't these heavenly?' She brandished them in front of Mike. 'They're from Luke.'

'From Luke?' Mike tried to sound casual but her heart missed a quick beat. How had he discovered that she was ill so quickly when the doctor had only just made his diagnosis? A diagnosis that had at least vindicated her assertion yesterday that she hadn't had too much to drink.

'Mmm.' Christina sat on the edge of the bed. 'It's to apologise for standing me up last night. Isn't that sweet of him?' Her eyes glowed.

'Very,' Mike muttered, irritated to realise how deflated she felt.

'Oh, Mike, I'm so sorry about the way I acted last night. Luke explained everything to me. I can see now that he didn't have any choice other than to look after you.' She giggled. 'He thought you were tipsy.'

'Yes, I know,' Mike said tightly.

'If only I'd known how ill you were, I wouldn't have been so horrible. Come to think of it, you did look dreadful.'

Mike's mouth curved wryly, and she decided that she was a little tired of hearing just how dreadful she looked. She was probably going to end up with a gigantic inferiority complex.

'Is there anything you want?' Christina asked earnestly, evidently anxious to make amends in a practical way.

'A glass of orange juice would be nice.' All she really wanted was to be left alone to be miserable in peace, but she didn't have the heart to disappoint Christina.

'I'll fetch it straight away.' The younger girl sprang to her feet. 'It's lucky I'm here to take care of you, isn't it?'

'It certainly is,' Mike agreed, hiding her sudden grin of amusement. The role of devoted nurse was one of which Christina would soon tire, of that she had no doubt.

But Mike was proved wrong. To her intense surprise, Christina seemed to be in her element over the following days, rushing around with endless trays sent up by Cook who appeared to have a curiously limited repertoire of invalid dishes. If she had boiled, baked or steamed fish followed by milk pudding for lunch one more time, she'd scream, Mike decided towards the end of the second week.

She wasn't the easiest of patients, she admitted. She disliked being fussed, being so dependent on other people, and, as she began to recover her strength, chafed rebelliously against the enforced inertia. She grew increasingly bored, unable to concentrate on the library books that Christina faithfully changed every few days, or the assortment of puzzles and jigsaws presented to her by other members of the household.

Instead she spent most of her time fretting about Kingston Air, thinking about Matthew... and about Luke. The frequency with which the image of a pair of grey, mocking eyes floated into her mind was disturbing.

He'd departed for Dorset two days after she'd been confined to bed, his business in London evidently successfully completed. He hadn't even bothered to put his head around the bedroom door to say goodbye before leaving, Mike remembered, merely relayed the usual platitudes for her recovery via Christina. Other than that she hadn't heard from him at all.

Until today. Mike stood by her bedroom window, fully dressed in a tailored cream suit, scowling at the letter in her hand. No, it wasn't even a letter, she amended ferociously. It was little more than a memo! She screwed up the piece of paper and threw it across the room.

'What are you doing? You're still supposed to be convalescing.' Christina entered the room carrying a breakfast tray. 'Mike?' she demanded, watching her elder sister stalk across the room and retrieve a canvas holdall from the wardrobe.

'I've spent most of the last fortnight in bed and I've had enough. I now pronounce myself fully recovered.' Mike began to throw an assortment of clothes into the bag. 'I'm going down to Rakers' and the airport today.' She'd already transported most of her possessions down to the house.

'But Mike——' Christina protested.

'Do you know what that man has done?' She zipped up the canvas bag savagely. 'Started to negotiate with the airport management committee for the handling contract! Without even consulting me first!'

'Calm down,' Christina ordered firmly and the sheer irony of the role reversals struck Mike so forcefully that she burst into laughter. Usually it was she who pacified Christina in a temper tantrum.

'What's the handling contract anyway? And you might just as well eat your breakfast now it's here.'

Her sense of humour restored, Mike sat down on her bedside chair. 'Not all the airlines that operate in and out of the airport have ground staff based there,' she started to explain. 'So their passengers are looked after by a handling agent.' She took a bite of toast, careful to avoid dropping crumbs on her suit. 'The airport authority renew the handling contract every five years.'

'And Luke's put in an application for Kingston Air to take over as handling agent?' Christina frowned with concentration and, seeing Mike's nod of affirmation, continued slowly, 'Well, I can't see what you're so steamed up about. It sounds a pretty sensible thing to do if it means more business for Kingston Air.'

Mike leapt to her feet. 'That's not the point! I'm supposed to be Luke's partner. He has no right to make such a major decision about the future of KA without me.' She picked up the holdall and slung it over her shoulder. 'You've been absolutely terrific this last fortnight, Chrissy.'

To Mike's surprise, her half-sister, never usually demonstrative, walked across the room and hugged her. 'Do you have to go this morning?' she asked wistfully. 'You could always see Luke tomorrow anyway. He's coming down to London for the day.'

'Is he?' Mike stiffened.

'Mmm. He telephoned last night when you were asleep and invited me out to lunch.'

Mike registered the information in silence, wondering why Christina hadn't blurted out the news earlier as would have been more characteristic. Neither did she appear unduly excited at the prospect of lunching with Luke. Perhaps she was disappointed that it wasn't a more romantic dinner engagement. A wave of anger and indignation tore through her. Luke hadn't found it necessary to telephone his business partner over the last two weeks, and yet he'd evidently found sufficient time to arrange his social life.

'I'd better go,' she muttered, moving towards the door, and then paused. 'Is something the matter?' Christina suddenly looked utterly forlorn and dejected.

'It's just that . . . I've been thinking . . .' Christina's voice trailed off into silence.

'Thinking what?' Mike prompted gently, hazel eyes clouding with puzzlement at the younger girl's unnatural reticence.

Christina shrugged. 'It doesn't matter. Not now anyway. You're in a rush.' She opened the bedroom door and walked out.

She should have waited and discovered what was troubling Christina, Mike thought guiltily as she sped down the motorway, the wind through the open window of the Porsche ruffling her auburn curls. It probably wasn't anything important, she consoled herself, and then frowned. That was hardly the point, was it? Vividly she recalled the number of occasions as a child when she'd desperately wanted to talk to her father about a problem which with the wisdom of hindsight had been trivial, but at the time had seemed insurmountable. But her father had always been too busy to listen, too involved with his business commitments. And wasn't she now beginning to fall into the same trap with Kingston Air? She would invite Christina down to Rakers' as soon as she was organised, she eased her conscience. But Christina had evidently needed someone *today* in whom to confide, a small voice reproached her. It was all Luke's fault, she thought savagely. If it weren't for him, there wouldn't be this urgency to tear down to the airport this morning.

The passenger terminal was crowded as Mike walked in, reminding her that Easter was fast approaching and with it the advent of the full, hectic summer programme. The two girls behind the Kingston Air check-in desk, looking immaculate in their uniform, were dealing courteously and efficiently with a long queue of passengers. A brief glance at the electronic information board confirmed that all the flights were running to schedule. Everything appeared to be operating smoothly and Mike was ashamed to discover that the knowledge irked her. She would have liked Luke to be encountering at least a few problems.

High heels clicking on the tiled floor, Mike walked briskly towards the Kingston Air offices. She pushed open the outer door and stopped, gazing incredulously around her. The walls of the corridor had been freshly emulsioned in brilliant white and a new grey carpet ran the length of the floor. The two walk-in cupboards that should have been on her immediate right had mysteriously vanished and in the space created by their removal was a small reception area.

A dark-haired girl sat behind a desk typing; aligned opposite her were two more girls and a young man, all three wearing distinctly apprehensive expressions.

'May I help you?' the brunette enquired with a courteous smile, looking up from her typing. Her smile vanished as Mike continued on down the corridor and flung open a door to the left. 'You can't go in there,' she protested, leaping to her feet. 'That's Mr Duncan's office.'

If Mike had hoped to disconcert Luke completely by her abrupt, unexpected entry, she was disappointed. Dark grey eyes revealed little more than minor surprise as he glanced up from the polished table and surveyed the slim, upright figure with the set face.

'Good morning, Michaelia,' he murmured with cool civility, rising to his feet. 'It's all right, Tina,' he added pleasantly to the dark-haired girl who had come dashing through the door after Mike and now stood looking bewildered. 'This is Miss Harrington.'

The girl flushed slightly. 'Oh, I didn't realise. I'm sorry.' She threw Mike a curious, slightly speculative glance.

'I'll let you know when I'm ready to see Miss Johnson,' Luke continued, consulting the list of names in front of him.

'Yes, Mr Duncan.' Flashing a brilliant smile, the girl retreated from the room.

'You should have let me know you were coming down to the airport today, Michaelia,' Luke said quietly as the door closed.

'So you could line up the new staff to greet me?' Mike enquired sweetly, the golden sparks in her eyes totally belying her sugary tone. There was a tightly coiled spring in the pit of her stomach threatening to snap at any moment. She paced over to the window and stared out. Losing her temper might release some of that anger curdling inside of her, might prove satisfying in the short term, but ultimately it would achieve very little. Thrusting her shaking hands deep into the pockets of her jacket, she turned round, her features schooled into an impassive mask.

'You have been busy,' she murmured coolly. 'I hardly recognised the place. Not even my own office.' Briefly her eyes wandered around the room; the faded yellow paint had been replaced by innocuous cream. She would have at least liked to have chosen her own décor, she seethed inwardly. 'I assume that this is still my office?' she added caustically.

'I'm only using it temporarily while mine's being decorated,' he returned easily.

Mike's whole attention had been concentrated on the powerful figure dominating the small room and it was only now that she became aware of the sounds of activity issuing from beyond the connecting door. It wasn't that she minded Luke using her office, she reasoned, trying to analyse that twisted feeling inside her. It was just that she would have preferred it if he'd had the courtesy to inform her of his intention to do so. She'd had sufficient shocks already this morning. To find Luke comfortably installed in her office, sitting behind her desk, seemed to be the final affront.

'What is Tina's function exactly?' she demanded. Other than to smile adoringly at her employer, she remembered witheringly. She was aware that she was quite deliberately avoiding the topic uppermost in her mind, the issue that had compelled her to come tearing down to the airport this morning. But right now she doubted her ability to discuss it rationally or objectively.

'I should have thought that was self-evident,' he answered drily. 'Receptionist and secretary. All the external telephone lines go through to Tina's switchboard now, and she redirects the calls as necessary. The operations staff have quite enough to do without answering fatuous questions from the general public.' He leaned back in his chair and linked his hands behind his head, the jacket of the dark grey suit tautening along the hard line of the muscular shoulders. 'She also monitors everyone who comes into the office, which seems to have successfully put a stop to half the airport wandering in and out whenever they felt like a coffee.'

'We're not running a prison camp,' Mike snapped.

'Neither are we operating a twenty-four-hour cafeteria service,' he retorted curtly. 'KA staff aren't employed to sit around drinking coffee with all and sundry, discussing the latest airport rumour.'

Mike fixed her eyes at a point above the dark head. His comment was perfectly justified, she admitted grudgingly. She herself had been aware of the growing tendency over the past weeks for airport personnel to congregate in the Kingston Air offices during their breaks and it was a problem she'd been planning to deal with. To discover that Luke had already solved it was infuriating. She lowered her gaze and saw him flick a quick, impatient glance at his wristwatch.

'I take it you're not in the process of holding auditions for the local amateur dramatics society?' she muttered, recalling the row of nervous faces in reception.

'One of the temps walked out the day before I arrived,' he informed her tersely. 'Hardly surprising considering no one seemed to have thought it necessary to train the girl. We're also going to need additional staff when we take over as handling agent.'

'When? Don't you mean if?' she demanded, her nails digging into the palm of her hand.

'The airport director contacted me earlier this morning. We've been offered the contract.' His mouth twisted. 'For heaven's sake sit down, Michaelia, or you'll wear a hole in the carpet!'

'Don't you dare tell me to sit down in my own damn office!' Mike flung back. 'You had no right to redecorate the offices without my consent let alone start negotiating for the——'

'I had every right,' he cut in grimly. 'I suggest that you read your partnership agreement again. In the advent of either partner being temporarily incapacitated, the other partner has full authority to make any decision he deems necessary.'

'I had flu, for Pete's sake,' Mike exploded. 'I wasn't lying in a coma in the middle of the Sahara.' There was absolutely no justification for not contacting her before today. 'Lines of communication do exist between here and London,' she said tartly. 'Ever heard of Alexander Graham Bell?'

'I telephoned you twice last week,' he said curtly, the line of his jaw hardening. 'And on each occasion I was informed that you still had a very high temperature and were in no condition to discuss anything.'

Weakly, Mike sank down into a chair. 'By my father?' she guessed, and sighed as she saw his nod of confirmation. How typical of her father to conveniently forget to tell her that Luke had called.

'The deadline for applying for the handling contract was this Monday. I had no alternative other than to go ahead without your knowledge.'

Of course he'd had an alternative, Mike thought wryly, but he'd chosen to ignore it. She flicked a glance at his face, noting for the first time the lines of weariness etched around his eyes, indicative of lack of sleep. He must have virtually lived at the airport for the past fortnight to have achieved so much in such a short space of time, she realised, but refused to feel either sympathy or admiration. There had been no need for Luke to drive himself so hard. As far as she was concerned, Kingston Air had managed without the handling contract for the last twenty years and would undoubtedly have continued to do so for the next twenty if Luke hadn't intervened. But he'd glimpsed an opportunity to expand the airline and hadn't been able to resist the challenge. Her eyes moved over the hard, irregular male features, and rested briefly on the square, tenacious jaw. He was just like her father, a relentlessly ambitious workaholic who would never be satisfied with the status quo.

'When do we actually take over the handling, then?' she asked resignedly.

'At the beginning of next month.' He shrugged. 'There are a couple of minor details to iron out and then we should sign the agreement after the weekend, on Monday.'

'We?' Hope flared in Mike's eyes. So it wasn't a complete *fait accompli* after all. 'You mean now I'm no longer "incapacitated", you'll need my consent to finalise the legalities?'

'Yes,' he said shortly, and, stretching out a lean hand retrieved a file from a tray on the table.

'Terms and conditions of the contract,' he said laconically. 'I'd intended to give you this tomorrow when I came to London.' He passed the file across to her and rose to his feet. 'Perhaps you'd like to read it as soon as possible.'

Before she had time to register what was happening, Mike found herself being ushered from the room.

'Incidentally,' he murmured as they stood in the doorway, 'I've upgraded Jean Evans and made her responsible for the training of all new recruits. I assume that you don't have any objections?'

'It's a bit late if I——' Mike started and then her mouth snapped shut in disbelief as she found herself addressing a firmly closed door. She had been dismissed from her own office—no, thrown out might be a more apt description! Luke hadn't even suggested that she sit in on the interviews, she realised incredulously—not that she had any strong inclinations to do so, she admitted honestly. Interviewing was a skill she had yet to acquire and she had no desire to make her first attempt at it under Luke's critical, watchful eyes.

She glanced down the corridor towards the hopeful candidates and her mouth curved in a sudden grin. A good-looking young man from the airport fire department was standing by the reception desk, talking animatedly to Tina. If Luke had been serious in his intention to stop casual callers wandering into the offices, he might have been better advised to have appointed a less attractive receptionist.

Slightly cheered up by the knowledge that Luke wasn't completely infallible, Mike walked towards the operations-room.

A scene of quiet, controlled activity met her eyes through the half-open door. Andrew Simpson was sitting behind a VDU screen, his fingers moving deftly over the keyboard as he transmitted a departure message on the last outbound aircraft; one of the duty officers was poring over a pile of paperwork, a frown of intense concentration on his face. Over in a corner the recently promoted senior girl was showing a newer member of staff how to fill in a property irregularity report, outlining the procedure for dealing with lost luggage should it arise. Totally absorbed in their tasks, no one noticed their silent observer.

Vividly Mike remembered the disorder that had greeted her on her last visit to the airport, recalled the general air of apathy that seemed to have pervaded the staff. The contrast between then and today couldn't have been more marked. In only two weeks, Luke had evidently made his impact. Kingston Air was operating as smoothly as when Matthew had been at the helm. Probably more so, Mike admitted grudgingly—the changes Luke had implemented were doubtless contributing to the airline's increased efficiency.

Abruptly, Mike turned and walked back down the corridor, clutching the file under her arm.

'If Mr Duncan wishes to contact me, I'll be at my home number,' she informed Tina crisply and continued out of the office door.

She smiled assuredly at the girls behind the check-in desk, exchanged pleasantries with one of the porters outside the terminal building, and called out a cheerful farewell to the car park attendant as she drove out of the airport. It wasn't until she was driving along the familiar country lanes towards Rakers' Moon that the mask slipped from her face and her eyes clouded dejectedly.

As she'd stood gazing into the operations-room, she'd suddenly felt like a complete outsider. She'd felt totally ineffectual, redundant, superfluous to all requirements. Her presence at the airport was so blatantly non-essential—Kingston Air was running like a well-oiled machine without her. On paper she might have equal status to Luke, but in practice it was he who had assumed command.

Nothing had turned out the way she'd planned it, Mike thought despondently. She'd come down to the airport prepared for battle, but Luke had neatly out-manoeuvred her every step of the way. He hadn't even had the courtesy to ask if she was fully recovered, she remembered bitterly.

Her eyes flicked quickly to the file lying on the seat beside her, containing all the details pertaining to the handling agreement. An agreement that she still had time to veto. Her eyes darkened thoughtfully. Wasn't it about time that Luke Duncan realised that he couldn't have everything his own way?

CHAPTER FOUR

SIGHING, Mike tossed the closed file on to the coffee-table drawn up beside the armchair in which she was curled. She'd spent all afternoon and a large part of the evening scrutinising the contents of the file, determined to find some condition or clause in the carefully constructed agreement to which she could object, and she'd had to acknowledge defeat. Unwillingly, she was forced to accept that the acquisition of the handling contract had been an astute business move and that Luke had skilfully negotiated the best possible terms for Kingston Air.

Unfurling her long, jeans-clad legs, Mike rose to her feet and switched on the standard lamp behind her chair. Barefooted, she padded across the drawing-room to the windows, looked out into the gathering dusk and then drew the heavy russet curtains together. She'd lit the log fire earlier, more for comfort than warmth, and the flames cast mysterious, flickering shadows over the walls.

Motionless, Mike stared into the fire and finally admitted the unpalatable truth. She could offer no sound argument for rejecting the handling agreement, and if she vetoed it at this late stage she would be doing so for personal and not business reasons, allowing her resentment towards Luke to impair her judgement completely.

She pulled a rueful face, unconsciously running a hand through her rumpled red curls. Instead of indulging in a petty power struggle with Luke, she ought to be thinking about the long-term future of the airline. Luke wasn't going to be at the airport forever. She should swallow her pride and take advantage of his presence over the next few weeks or months to learn as much as she could from him, preparing herself for the day when she would be left in sole charge. She grimaced. The role of humble pupil was not one that greatly appealed, she thought gloomily.

She stiffled a sudden yawn and glanced at the ornate clock on the mantelpiece. It was about time she prepared herself some supper, she supposed.

She walked down the long hall, flicking on lights as she went, and entered a large, square room, that, despite the installation of modern, time-saving equipment, still managed to retain the air of an old-fashioned, homely farmhouse kitchen. Without much enthusiasm, Mike contemplated the eggs and assortment of salad vegetables she'd earlier purchased from the farm shop down the lane. She'd have a more comprehensive shopping expedition tomorrow, she decided, fishing out an apron from a drawer and slipping it over her head to protect her cream cashmere jumper.

It wasn't until she had arrived at the empty house that morning that she'd remembered that John and his wife, the only residential staff, were under the impression that she wouldn't be moving down to Rakers' Moon until after the weekend as had been her original intention, and were taking a short holiday in Sussex, visiting their daughter.

'Scrambled or omelette?' Mike asked herself out loud as she cracked two eggs into a glass bowl and then grinned shamefacedly. It was the first time she'd ever been entirely alone in the huge old house and she was beginning to find the silence oppressive, the longing to hear another human voice disturbingly acute. She had become accustomed to the clatter of her half-brothers and sisters charging noisily around their London home, she decided, beating the eggs with a fork. It wasn't until this evening, either, that she'd realised just how isolated was Rakers' Moon. The darkness beyond the uncurtained kitchen window was absolute, unrelieved by any reassuring lights from close neighbours. Absently, Mike poured the contents of the bowl into a pan on the stove. Someone could come creeping up to the house, camouflaged by that shroud of blackness, and she wouldn't even know they were there until...

The glass bowl slipped from her hands and crashed to the floor as the peal of the doorbell echoed around the empty house. Furiously, Mike glared down at the fragments of glass. Anyone would think she was nervous...

She turned on the porch light and peered through the hall window, unashamed relief flooding through her as she recognised the tall figure standing on the doorstep.

'One-hour working day going to be the norm from now on?' Luke greeted her unceremoniously, walking uninvited into the hall.

Mike looked up at him calmly, determined not to bite. The grey suit, the tie loosened at the neck of his shirt, the dark shadow around his jaw made her suspect that he had come straight from the airport, but she refused to feel guilty. No one forced him to work such unnecessary long hours.

'I came home to read through the handling contract,' she informed him coolly, wishing that she hadn't forgotten to replace her shoes and remove the apron. It was a definite psychological disadvantage

in any confrontation to be barefoot and clad in a
plastic apron adorned with airborne pink and green
elephants. 'Assuming the contents of the file you gave
me were confidential,' she continued, 'I could hardly
go and sit in the crew-room or staff canteen to read
them.' Never would she admit to those feelings of in-
adequacy that had assailed her that morning and
prompted her rapid departure from the airport. 'My
office was already occupied, if you recall,' she added
sweetly. She frowned, puzzled by the expression on
Luke's face and then her own nostrils were assailed
by the smell of burning.

'Oh, heavens, my scrambled eggs!' she yelped and
sped down the hall to the kitchen.

She removed the pan from the stove and inspected
the contents mournfully.

'Fending for yourself tonight, I see,' Luke drawled
from the doorway, his eyes moving from the burnt,
congealed mass in the saucepan to the fragments of
broken glass strewn across the floor.

'I'm quite capable of...' Mike started tetchily and
then paused. Why did she always assume that he was
being derogatory, deliberately look for implied criticism in his every remark? She wasn't usually so touchy
and sensitive. She'd never minded being teased about
her shortcomings by her fellow engineers, and yet
when she was with Luke she seemed to lose her sense
of humour completely.

She gave a reluctant grin. 'I'm not the world's most
proficient cook,' she admitted. She'd learned the
basics at school but, having always lived in a
household with a resident cook, had seldom needed
to put those skills into practice.

Luke surveyed the remaining eggs on top of the
refrigerator.

'My omelettes are the toast of Manhattan,' he murmured modestly.

'You must be very proud,' Mike returned gravely, her eyes dancing with amusement. She swept an arm in the direction of the stove. 'It's all yours,' she informed him generously.

'Bowl? Frying-pan?' he enquired, tossing his jacket over a pine stool and folding back the sleeves of his shirt.

'In the cupboard over there.' She was taken aback, hadn't expected him to take her flippant offer seriously, wasn't even certain that she wanted him to prepare their simple, communal supper.

Her forehead furrowed. What was Luke doing here anyway? He'd offered no real explanation for his unexpected visit. She somehow doubted that he'd driven all the way over here, tired and hungry after a long day, merely to accuse her of slacking!

'Where are you staying at the moment?' she asked with sudden curiosity, leaning back against the sink unit. 'At the Smuggler's Rest?'

He quirked an eyebrow at her. 'Didn't I tell?' he murmured infuriatingly. 'I'm your new neighbour. I've rented the farm cottage down the lane.'

'Oak Tree Cottage?' Mike exclaimed in disbelief. The cottage, the tree from which its name originated long since felled, was barely half a mile away from Rakers' Moon. No longer used to house farm labourers, it was let out to holiday-makers during the summer months, but usually remained empty in the winter. It had never occurred to her that the cottage was already occupied this early in the season . . . let alone that the tenant was Luke!

'Hadn't you better go and put some shoes on and pick up that glass before you cut your feet?'

He was giving her orders in her own home now, Mike observed with a mixture of amusement and rancour. Shrugging, she went to retrieve her sandals from the drawing-room, and, returning to the kitchen, crouched down on the tiled floor and began to collect the glass up in a dustpan, watching Luke from under her dark lashes as she did so.

Whistling softly under his breath, he looked relaxed and completely at ease as with controlled, economical movements he went around the kitchen collecting utensils.

'Ouch!' Mike looked at the blood oozing from her finger in exasperation. She ought to have been concentrating on her task instead of watching Luke. She walked quickly over to the sink and held her right hand under the running tap.

'Could you give me a plaster, please?' she addressed Luke over her shoulder. 'There should be some in the first-aid tin by the dresser.'

'Give me your hand,' he murmured, coming up behind her, and with unexpected gentleness he applied the plaster to her outstretched finger.

The physical contact between them was minimal, but Mike was appalled to discover that her pulse-rate seemed to have doubled. Her eyes were drawn to his hands, fascinated by the lean, supple fingers, the short, surgically clean nails.

'Thank you,' she murmured, her voice not quite steady as he completed his administrations.

He didn't release her hand immediately but with great deliberation raised it to his mouth, touching the tip of her wounded finger with his lips.

'Occupational therapy?' Mike enquired drily, her heart hammering so loudly that she was sure he would hear it. Ye gods, she'd never realised just how erogenous was the sensitive skin at the end of her fingers.

'We may as well eat in the drawing-room,' she murmured casually, moving away from him, and busied herself preparing two trays, willing her erratic heartbeat to return to normal. The imaginary menace lurking out in the darkness now seemed laughable. The threat to her peace of mind was much closer at hand.

The omelette was excellent, Mike admitted, nursing her empty plate on her lap. Not that she had doubted for a second that it would be. Luke, she was certain, wasn't a man given to idle boasts, even those made in jest.

Her eyes drifted across the room to where he was sitting on the sofa in front of the fire, his long legs stretched out in front of him, his arms folded with deceptive indolence across his chest. The flickering flames threw shadows across the planes of his face, the glow from the single lamp softening the craggy contours.

He turned his head and smiled across at her. Mike's stomach muscles contracted involuntarily. That unexpected slow, lazy smile still managed to catch her off guard.

'What's your verdict? On the handling agreement?' he added, the teasing note in the deep voice making her suspect that he had been aware of her intense scrutiny.

'The terms seem acceptable enough,' she answered, her voice as expressionless as her face. It was churlish of her not to sound more enthusiastic, she admitted. After all his hard work, she could have at least congratulated him on his success.

'So we can go ahead with formalities on Monday?'

'Why not?' She shrugged. She saw the sudden gleam in his dark eyes and had the uncomfortable feeling that he had guessed at the inner battle she'd raged with herself all afternoon. Was she that transparent? she wondered uneasily. 'How did the interviews go?' Quickly she moved on to a safer topic of conversation.

'One girl seems suitable. She's had previous airline experience which is a decided advantage.' He paused. 'Would you like her to come back for a second interview so you can meet her?'

'No.' It would be a waste of time, but she was gratified that he'd made the suggestion, hadn't simply gone ahead and made the appointment without consulting her first. 'I trust your judgement,' she said lightly, making her own peace-offering.

'We're going to need at least three more staff,' he murmured. 'Perhaps you could contact the agency tomorrow and arrange some further interviews for next week? Oh, and remind Tina to send off letters to the unsuccessful candidates.' He crossed one leg casually over a knee, his trousers tautening along the line of his muscular thighs. 'And could you chase up Stantons? Reservations are running low on domestic tickets.'

'Anything else?' Mike asked drily, resisting the temptation to touch a forelock. It was quite obvious now why Luke had called in this evening—to give her a list of orders for tomorrow. He was treating her as little more than his assistant, she realised with growing exasperation.

'One other thing,' he continued smoothly. 'I think we ought to call a meeting of the senior staff as soon as possible and fill them in on the handling contract. Could you try and organise it for tomorrow evening?

About seven, after the last outbound flight. I should be back from London by then.'

Mike didn't answer but rose abruptly to her feet, deciding that it might be politic to escape to the kitchen for a while, before she said something she might later regret.

'I'll make some coffee,' she murmured, collecting the empty plates. At least she wouldn't feel redundant tomorrow, she thought wryly.

She heard the sound of music floating down the hall as she emerged from the kitchen, clasping two mugs of coffee. 'Do make yourself at home,' she muttered caustically under her breath, automatically assuming that Luke had turned on the radio or television. She nudged open the drawing-room door with her shoulder and her eyes darkened with amazement.

Luke was seated at the piano at the far end of the room, his fingers moving over the ivory keys. Tchaikovsky, she guessed accurately. Even to her own untrained ears, it was obvious that she was listening to someone with far more than just average ability. She was transfixed, her eyes riveted to Luke's absorbed face, the haunting music washing over her, drawing out a web of confused emotions from deep inside her. One moment she felt exhilarated, happy, and the next she was torn apart by sadness.

He glanced up and the spell was broken, the tempo of the music changing, the tune catchy but unfamiliar.

'What's that?' Mike walked silently across the carpet, drawn irresistibly towards the piano.

'You're listening to the first public rendition of a Duncan original score,' he informed her with mock solemnity, and to her disappointment stopped playing. She could have listened to him all night.

He swivelled around on the stool and faced her. 'Do you mind?' he asked quietly, quirking an eyebrow at the piano. 'I couldn't resist it.'

'Of course not,' Mike said quickly, handing him a coffee. She wanted to tell him to come and use the piano whenever he wanted, but didn't feel sufficiently at ease with him to make the offer. She would hate him to misconstrue the invitation, to think that she had some ulterior motive in extending it. 'Matthew used to play,' she continued, and then added with simple honesty, 'He wasn't in your league though.'

'I once considered becoming a professional musician,' he said carelessly, sipping his coffee.

'Why did you change your mind?' Her tone was casual but her eyes rested intently on his face. She was beginning to realise just how little she really knew about this increasingly enigmatic man.

He didn't answer. 'Can you play "Chopsticks"?' he asked instead.

Mike shrugged. 'Matthew taught me when I was a child.' She felt snubbed because he had deliberately evaded her question. 'I haven't played for ages though.'

'Come on, see what you can remember,' he murmured persuasively, taking the mug out of her hand and placing it with his own on a table. He returned to the piano, deliberately making room for her beside him on the stool.

'Come on,' he repeated with an encouraging grin, dark eyes on her reluctant face.

As usual it was his smile that was her undoing—it made her weaken and give in to his request.

'Why not?' she murmured with a nonchalance she was far from feeling. She sat down next to him, instantly regretting it as her slender hips encountered a hard band of muscle. This stool had most emphatically not been designed to accommodate two—the lower halves of their bodies were practically cemented together.

'Ready?'

She nodded, not daring to look directly at him. Her hands began to fumble over the keys, her fingers stiff and awkward.

'You're not concentrating,' Luke admonished her. 'And if you're not careful you're going to fall off the edge of the stool.'

'I told you I'm out of practice,' Mike snapped, her nerves as taut as a wire. 'You're going far too quickly for me.' She stopped playing. 'I can't remember any more anyway.'

Before she had time to protest, warm strong hands covered her own smaller ones, guiding her fingers across the keys. If her fingers had been clumsy and stiff before, they were now frozen rigid.

'Relax,' he murmured softly. 'This is supposed to be fun.'

She could feel his breath on her cheek and, turning her head, discovered that his face was barely inches from her own. His hand moved from hers, and slid inside the sleeve of her jumper, the long fingers languidly stroking the sensitive, delicate skin of her forearms. Her eyes locked into dark grey shadowy depths and a warning bell clanged in her head. It was imperative that she extricate herself from this potentially dangerous situation as swiftly as possible.

She jumped to her feet but was thwarted in her escape. The pressure of Luke's hand on her arm increased and he pulled her down on to his lap. One hand curved around the nape of her neck, tilting her face up towards his. The other snaked around her hips, drawing her even closer against his body.

'Now, this could be even more fun,' he murmured, his mouth brushing tantalisingly against her lips before moving to imprint sensuous little kisses over her temples and cheekbones. Shock waves tingled up Mike's spine. Her eyes closed as his mouth took possession of hers again, her arms moving up instinctively around his neck, her hands curling through the thick dark hair.

'Now, this could be even more fun.' The words suddenly burnt into her brain. The tenderness in that warm, seductive mouth was a sheer hypocrisy. Luke was simply amusing himself with her. A burst of adrenalin surged through her. Rebelliously, she compressed her lips together, refusing to allow the deeper intimacy Luke was now seeking, fighting against the sweet, drugging pleasure that threatened to engulf her completely, and make her lose all reason.

Did this man think he had unrestricted licence to touch her, to kiss her whenever he chose? With all her strength, Mike pushed against the hard wall of his chest and wriggled free of his embrace.

'Do you make a habit of kissing all your business associates?' she demanded with an iciness that was in direct conflict to her burning, inflamed cheeks. Her small, rounded breasts rose and fell in time with her erratic breathing as she confronted Luke.

'Is that my cue to say only the beautiful ones with red hair and the most irresistible freckles?' he drawled as he rose to his feet, his hand moving to her waist as he implanted a swift kiss on the tip of her nose.

Mike flung his hand away. 'No, it's your cue to say goodnight and go home!' Her mouth curled disdainfully. Did he think that she was trying to flirt with him? That she welcomed his casual, meaningless caresses?

She stalked across the room and flung open the door. 'I believe your jacket is still in the kitchen. Don't forget to collect it on your way out.' The freezing hauteur on her face had quelled more than one amorous attempt by hopeful, intoxicated young men at her father's parties, but it seemed to have no such effect on Luke. Instead he was looking at her with unconcealed amusement.

'Have dinner with me tomorrow night, Michaelia. After the staff meeting.'

She gazed up at him incredulously. He was unbelievable. The utter nerve of the man! He'd invited Christina to lunch tomorrow and now he was trying to arrange a dinner date with her for the same day. Who did he have lined up to share his breakfast with? she wondered caustically.

'No, thanks,' she said sweetly.

He shrugged his broad shoulders, and made no effort to persuade her to change her mind, seemingly unconcerned by her refusal.

Mike waited until he had fetched his jacket from the kitchen and then, keeping a safe distance, followed him to the front door.

'See you tomorrow evening, Michaelia.'

She tensed, expecting him to try and kiss her again but he made no attempt to do so. He started to walk down the wide steps and then paused, swinging back round to face her, his eyebrows drawn together in a frown.

'Will you be all right in the house on your own?' he asked abruptly.

She was taken aback by the seriousness in both his eyes and voice. She simply couldn't fathom out this baffling man. An arrogant, ruthless, cynical man who was nevertheless capable of playing the piano with such feeling that it could almost reduce her to tears; a man who, judging by his single status and reputation as a playboy, was incapable of committing himself to any one woman. And yet he was now looking at her as if her welfare was of the utmost importance to him . . . as if she genuinely mattered to him . . .

'I'll be fine,' she finally muttered.

'Well, you know where I am if you get lonely,' he drawled.

'Don't lose any sleep waiting for my call,' she advised him drily. How easily she'd been duped by that apparent concern in his eyes. Asking her if she minded being alone in the house had simply been a line—and she'd so nearly fallen for it. If she'd been foolish enough to confess to her ridiculous fears, she could just imagine the remedy he would have suggested.

She watched him stride away into the darkness and slammed the front door shut, bolting it securely. As she wandered back into the drawing-room, she heard the sound of the powerful car fading into the distance. She slumped down on the sofa. Now Luke had gone, the house seemed even more deathly quiet. She leapt to her feet and began to prowl around the room restlessly, inspecting the well-stocked bookcase, before finally coming to rest in front of the piano. She stood there for a long time, gazing down at the keyboard, her eyes dark with confused thoughts.

Mike glanced at the clock on the wall. Luke would be on the motorway now, approaching London.

'Come in,' she murmured in response to the tap at the office door.

'Where I shall put these?' Tina appeared clutching a pile of letters. 'They need Mr Duncan's signature before I can send them off.'

'If you'd like to leave them here, please, I'll sign them,' Mike said easily.

With evident reluctance, Tina placed them on the desk and then paused uncertainly. 'If anybody phones to speak to Mr Duncan today, shall I tell them he's not here?'

'Just put the calls through to me,' Mike said patiently and grinned wryly as the door closed. It was evident where the young receptionist's allegiance lay. She was clearly unhappy about Mike's presence in what she obviously regarded as Luke's domain.

Mike started to read through the letters, and then looked up as she was interrupted a second time. She smiled at the silver-haired man, the gold braid on the sleeves and epaulettes of his dark jacket signifying his rank as captain, who walked into the office in response to her summons.

'Luke about?' he asked casually.

'He's in London for the day,' Mike explained. 'Can I help?'

She saw the hesitation on his face. 'Not to worry, I'll catch Luke tomorrow. I only wanted to ask him if there was any chance of taking two days' leave next week.' He started to turn away and Mike felt a wave of frustration tear through her. Why did everyone seem to assume that it was only Luke who had the authority to make decisions?

'I'll have a look at the roster,' she said swiftly before he reached the door, 'and see what I can do.'

He paused. 'Right. Thanks. He smiled. 'I'm sorry, Mike, I was forgetting that you——'

'Yes, I know,' she cut in drily. 'Pop in and see me when you get back from Alderney.'

It wasn't until she started to juggle with the roster, swopping the crews around, trying out various permutations, that Mike realised that her task wasn't as straightforward as she'd imagined.

She had to be careful to ensure that none of the flight deck crew worked more than the legal number of hours and had the statutory rest periods between flights. She had to make allowances for possible delays—the crews' hours were determined from the time they came on duty and not the time they were actually airborne. She didn't want a situation where an aircraft was stuck in Glasgow or the Isle of Man with an out of hours crew, unable to fly the return sector. It didn't help matters that one of the first officers was already on leave the following week.

There was one way of granting the requested leave but that would mean leaving two early morning flights without a full standby crew. Should she risk it? She grimaced. What happened if someone fell unexpectedly sick or there were extensive delays?

'I'm sorry,' she apologised to the captain when he returned for her answer later that morning. 'It's not possible, I'm afraid.' It was her first real decision, she realised, albeit a very minor one.

He shrugged resignedly. 'Didn't think there was much chance, actually. I should have put in for the leave earlier, but my daughter only telephoned last night to say that she was bringing my two grandchildren down to stay with us for a couple of days at the beginning of the Easter holidays. It would have been nice to have taken them all out for the day somewhere, but not to worry.'

'How old are your grandchildren?' Mike asked, thinking rapidly.

'Eight and ten.'

She glanced briefly at the roster again. 'You're operating the Guernsey flight on Wednesday. If there are seats available, I'll authorise two sub-load tickets for the children.'

'Thanks very much, Mike. They'll be thrilled to bits.'

Mike watched him walk out the door, doubts beginning to assail. Should she have offered him two discounted tickets to which he wasn't strictly speaking entitled? It had been Matthew's policy, and, since she and Luke hadn't discussed it, was presumably still company policy that only employees of Kingston Air, their spouses, parents or children were eligible for concessionary staff travel. She frowned. Surely it didn't hurt to stretch the rules slightly for once?

She glanced at her wristwatch. Luke would have arrived at his London office by now.

The internal telephone summoned her attention and she picked it up quickly, recognising the brisk voice of the reservations supervisor, an efficient, down-to-earth woman in her early fifties.

'Mike, we're up to our eyes in it at the moment,' she said without preamble. 'Julie's off sick, there are dozens of tickets on departure to prepare for this afternoon's flights, accounts are screaming for the weekly ticket summary and the telephone's never stopped ringing. Any chance of sending someone on from Ops or Traffic to help out?'

There were no strong demarcation lines within Kingston Air. Matthew had insisted that all the ground staff had a basic grounding in traffic, operational and reservation procedure, enabling one department to provide cover for another if necessary.

Matthew, Mike recalled, had been prepared to undertake any task himself if the need arose, even the most menial.

'I'll come and give you a hand,' Mike offered. She had nothing of great urgency to attend to in her office, had already carried out Luke's thinly disguised orders of the night before, and would welcome an opportunity to gain more reservation experience. She'd attended a short reservation and domestic ticketing course run by one of the major airlines in London for her own satisfaction, but had so far little chance to put theory into practice. Matthew had been proficient in all fields and she was determined to emulate him.

Quickly, she dialled the number of the reception desk. 'Tina, I shall be in the reservations office if anyone needs me.'

'Yes, Miss Harrington.'

Mike soon became engrossed in her new task, operating the computer cautiously at first and then with growing confidence, only occasionally needing to consult the reservations manual. Most of the calls were from travel agents, some simply wanting to check the availability on certain flights for indecisive clients, others requesting firm bookings. Some of the bookings involved onwards connections with other international carriers, and these Mike passed over to more experienced staff, unfamiliar with the procedure for constructing international fares. It was an area she would have to gen up on, she reminded herself.

She took a short break at one o'clock, hastily eating a sandwich in the canteen. Luke would probably be ensconced in some small, intimate restaurant with Christina by now. Did he have further business to attend to this afternoon, or was he planning to spend the time with Christina? An unwanted image of Luke smiling down into her half-sister's eyes floated un-invited into Mike's head, giving her an uncomfortable and unexpected jolt.

The pressure in the reservations office eased by late afternoon and she decided to return to Rakers' Moon for a couple of hours before the staff meeting. She'd been at the airport since seven and was beginning to fell tired and decidedly grubby. Luke couldn't accuse her of slacking today, she thought wryly. What time would he arrive back from London?

His car wasn't in the car park when she returned to the airport in the early evening. She'd changed out of her businesslike tailored navy suit into a soft cream woollen dress, one of her favourites. She had never been attracted to ornate, fussy clothes, preferring them to be simple and well cut. She'd added two pearl drop earrings and varnished her nails the same subtle shade of pink as her lip gloss, wondering as she'd done so why she was taking quite so much trouble with her appearance for a staff meeting.

She sat in her office, pretending to read through the reservations manual, her ears tuned for the sound of brisk footsteps coming down the corridor, the sound of a certain familiar, deep voice. There was a knotted sensation in the pit of her stomach. She'd experienced the same edgy, wound-up feeling just before an exam, or when she was waiting outside the dentist's surgery. Surely she wasn't apprehensive about seeing Luke again? Where on earth was he anyway? He was cutting it a bit fine now and she had no desire to hold the meeting on her own.

The door opened and Mike was shocked by the rush of warm pleasure that swamped over her as she looked up into the dark craggy face, hoping desperately that her eyes weren't betraying the confusion inside her.

'What are all these people doing in the ops-room at this time of the evening?' he growled, without even greeting her. He strode across the carpet and came to a halt in front of the desk.

'Hello, Luke. Had a good day?' Mike murmured sweetly. Did he have to glower at her like that for no apparent reason? He must have returned to the cottage to shower and shave before coming to the airport, she decided, her nostrils assailed by the subtle tang of expensive aftershave, mingled with the more disturbing scent of clean, soapy male skin.

'I thought Ops would be the best place to hold the meeting as it's the biggest office,' Mike continued, answering his question. 'I asked all the staff to attend, by the way,' she added casually. 'After all, the handling contract is going to affect everyone.'

'You've done what?' He groaned. 'I suspected as much when I walked in.' His eyes narrowed. 'I thought we agreed that the meeting should be confined to the senior staff.'

'*We* didn't agree to anything,' Mike reminded him stiffly. Why did he look so irritable and angry? Perhaps it was simply because she hadn't obeyed his orders to the letter.

'Well, it's too damn late to do anything about it now,' he muttered tersely, glancing at his wristwatch. He swung around on his heels and strode back towards the door. 'But for Pete's sake, think things through first in future before you give way to your democratic urges,' he barked over his shoulder as he vanished into the corridor.

'And what's that supposed to mean?' Mike demanded of the empty office, rising to her feet. Pondering on Luke's ambiguous remark, she made her way to the operations-room.

She'd just automatically taken it for granted that it would be Luke who conducted the meeting, Mike realised, as she sat listening to him outlining the changes that were about to take place within Kingston Air to his attentive audience.

She'd rather over-simplified the role of the handling agent when she'd explained it to Christina. Kingston Air wasn't simply going to be responsible for handling other airlines' passengers, but also for manning the airport information desk, collecting landing fees from private pilots, organising duty frees from the bonded store for the latter, keeping a record of all the freight placed in the transit shed to await Customs clearance. The list was endless and it was going to mean a lot of extra work for the staff and yet they greeted Luke's announcement with open enthusiasm. They were responding to Luke as they would have done to Matthew, Mike realised, wondering wryly what their reaction would have been if she'd been the one to impart the news.

She glanced around the crowded room. Despite the short notice, all the staff were in attendance, even those who had finished their shifts at two o'clock that afternoon for their precious weekend off.

Luke was now answering the barrage of eager questions being fired at him and as she listened to his calm, assured voice Mike suddenly felt a fierce rush of pride in him, which she instantly dismissed as absurd. She had no right to feel such an emotion—and neither did she want to!

Her gaze fell on Andrew Simpson, sitting alone at the back of the room, and she cringed inwardly as she witnessed the bitter curl of his mouth, the unconcealed resentment in his eyes. Oh, God, she should have done exactly as Luke had requested, called a meeting of senior staff only. How could she have been so utterly thoughtless as to allow Andrew to learn about the airline's new venture at exactly the same time as the most junior, temporary staff? No wonder he was angry and resentful.

She heard a ripple of laughter echo around the room and realised that Luke must have closed the meeting on a humorous note. Quickly, she leaped out of the room and escaped to her office. Sitting down at her desk, she rested her head in her hands, feeling sick with shame, appalled by her insensitivity towards Andrew.

'I don't normally reduce my audiences to quite such a level of despondency,' a voice drawled from the doorway.

Mike looked up. 'Did you see Andrew's face?' she asked abruptly.

'Yes,' he answered quietly.

'You were right, Luke,' she muttered miserably. 'We should have talked to the senior personnel first. I shouldn't have interfered.' Her eyes darkened. 'I've been so crass, so unbelievably stupid.'

She waited for him to endorse her statement, embellish it with a few well-chosen adjectives of his own, and was nonplussed when he merely studied her for a moment in silence, the expression on his face unreadable, and then gave an unexpected smile.

'You know, I don't think sackcloth and ashes suit you, Michaelia,' he murmured thoughtfully. 'Come on, I'll walk you to your car.'

Wondering if she'd ever be able to comprehend this unpredictable man, ever understand how his mind worked, Mike collected her jacket and handbag.

There were people milling about in the terminal as they walked through, waiting to meet arrivals off the last inbound flights of the day, and Mike observed the number of female heads that turned to appraise her companion. She flicked a sideways glance up at him, curious to see his reaction. But he gave no indication that he was even aware of the attention he was attracting. Perhaps he was so accustomed to drawing female eyes wherever he went that it no longer even registered with him, she mused. She wondered if he had any idea that, perversely, it was that very air of indifference and cool aloofness that made him even more compelling to women. Some women, she amended hastily, having no wish to include herself in that generalisation.

'Incidentally, I'm going to be up in London for the day again tomorrow,' Luke announced casually as they reached Mike's car.

'Are you?' she murmured vaguely, staring down at the ground. Did he have more business to attend to? She frowned. On a Saturday? Or was he simply going to see Christina again?

'If you come to work tomorrow, I'll cover on Sunday and you can have the day off,' he continued. 'If that suits you,' he added as an afterthought, as if belatedly remembering that she wasn't one of his employees.

Mike shrugged. 'I might as well come in on Sunday as well.' She'd hardly worked her full quota this week and she'd had quite sufficient leisure time over the past fortnight anyway.

'I should make the most of Sunday,' he retorted firmly. 'I doubt whether either of us are going to have much free time over the next couple of weeks. There's still a great deal of preparation to do before we take over the handling at the beginning of the month.'

'OK.' She couldn't be bothered to argue. And neither was she in the mood to stand here talking about business. In fact, she was becoming heartily sick of the handling contract. She unlocked the car door and slid into the driver's seat. 'See you on Monday, then.'

With a feeling of complete anticlimax, she watched Luke walk away. She'd been so convinced that he was going to ask her out to dinner again after the staff meeting! Wasn't that the real reason she'd taken so much trouble with her appearance, in anticipation of such an invitation? she asked herself mockingly.

She turned the ignition key. Why *should* Luke repeat his dinner invitation when she'd refused it point-blank last night? Some men, she knew from experience, might have regarded her professed disinterest as a direct challenge, but Luke was not apparently in that catagory.

Mechanically, she started on her homeward journey. She'd had a few boyfriends over the years and had always been completely honest and straightforward with them, never leading them to suppose that she wanted anything more from then than a light, casual friendship. She wasn't capricious by nature, wasn't prone to prevarication. When she'd refused an invitation in the past, she'd always meant it and had been profoundly irritated when the man who had extended it had persisted with his unwanted attentions, seeming to assume either that she was incapable of knowing her own mind, or alternatively that she was deliberately indulging in some devious game, all part of a feminine strategy to maintain his interest. So why did she now feel so deflated and disappointed that Luke had taken her at her word and made no effort to change her mind?

She changed into jeans and a sweatshirt the moment she arrived at Rakers' Moon, anxious to discard the cream dress that was a constant, pricking reminder of her own foolishness. No longer hungry, she heated up a tin of soup and then retreated to the drawing-room with a book by one of her favourite authors. She'd been planning to telephone Christina tonight, but was oddly reluctant to do so any more. Half of her wanted to know if her suspicions were correct and that Luke had arranged to see her half-sister tomorrow—and the other half preferred not to know.

Finding she couldn't concentrate on her novel, she flung it aside and on a sudden impulse leapt to her feet, rushed into the hall and tore up the stairs to the top of the house.

From one of the attic windows, she had an un-trammelled view of the lane leading down to Oak Tree Cottage. Craning her neck, she rested her elbows on the window-sill and gazed out. The cottage lay in complete darkness. So Luke hadn't gone straight home from the airport. Had he driven back down to London tonight? Or simply found another dinner companion?

A wave of self-disgust tore through her. She was acting like an adolescent with a crush on the boy next door, standing here in the darkness, staring out at Luke's cottage. Abruptly, she turned away from the window and flicked on the light switch. Never in her life had she indulged in such humiliating behaviour. But then, she admitted, with a thud of her heart, this was the first time she'd ever encountered a man like Luke Duncan.

She walked over to a large wooden packing-crate and sat down. It was time she faced the truth, was honest at least with herself. Her mind might tell her that she was immune to Luke's blatant maleness, but she only had to be in the same room as he and her traitorous, wilful hormones would denounce her as a liar.

Absently, she traced a circle on the dusty floor with the toe of her shoe. This was a complication she could well do without, she thought wryly, and it was a problem she was going to have to resolve. Even if Luke's interest in her had been more than a brief, transitory physical one, even if he weren't the type of man with whom she long ago vowed never to become emotionally involved with, she would never contemplate a relationship of any sort with a man who was her business partner. It would be a recipe for disaster. The old adage about never mixing business with pleasure might be hackneyed but it was founded on common sense.

From now on, Mike resolved determinedly, she would ensure that she never saw Luke socially, limit their contact to a working environment, and their conversation to business. Never again would she allow herself to get into a situation, as she had last night, that could so easily have become out of control. It wasn't Luke she feared, she admitted uncomfortably, but herself. It was becoming increasingly difficult to fight her instinctive response to him.

She stood up, wiping her dusty hands on her jeans, and heaved a despondent sigh. She'd been so looking forward to moving down to Rakers' Moon and working at the airport and now nothing seemed to be turning out the way she'd planned. The future that had once beckoned challengingly now loomed with bleak dreariness.

CHAPTER FIVE

'WHAT the hell are you trying to do Michaelia? Put Kingston Air out of business?'

Mike didn't answer, watching Luke from under her thick eyelashes as he paced up and down the office, his face like thunder.

'Have you any idea of how much it costs to keep re-routeing passengers via Heathrow? Not to mention the damage that's being done to Kingston Air's reputation.'

Mike closed her mind to Luke's angry tirade, letting his words wash over her head. She was beginning to feel as if she were in a nightmare, a nightmare that had started on Monday when two regular business travellers had arrived at the check-in desk, holding valid tickets for the early morning departure to Manchester, to be courteously informed that their names weren't on the passenger list for the full flight. A check with the computer had revealed that although the two men had originally been booked on the flight their seats had subsequently been cancelled and re-booked for the following week, a change in itinerary both irate men had vehemently denied requesting.

Mike's eyes darkened. The same confusion had occurred later that day on a Jersey flight, yesterday on flights to Paris and Alderney, and now this morning there had been yet another false cancellation on the Glasgow flight. Mike's hands clenched into tight fists. And each time the computer had indicated that it was she who had been guilty of altering the passengers' itineraries. She was beginning to dread coming into work, to dread the moment when the office door opened and she heard Luke's frozen voice accusing her of committing yet another reservations blunder.

'What I fail to understand is what possessed you to go and help out in Res in the first place. Why the hell didn't you send someone in from Ops who at least had some idea of what they were doing?'

Mike's eyes flashed amber sparks. 'For the umpteenth time,' she said evenly, trying hard to keep the mounting anger and frustration from her voice, 'I did not make all these mistakes.' She saw the deep scepticism in his eyes. 'What exactly do you think I did on Friday?' she demanded caustically. 'Brought up passenger lists for every flight this week and methodically worked my way through them, modifying bookings just for the fun of it?' She took a gulp of air. 'Changing a whole itinerary involves a little more than simply pressing one key. It's not something you can do by accident, and I'd hardly to it deliberately!'

'You already know how I think the errors occurred,' Luke growled back. 'You admit yourself that you had a quick practice on the computer, experimenting with various bookings, before you——'

'I did that using the training sign,' Mike cut in exasperatedly. 'Nothing would have entered the system.' She sighed wearily. This was getting nowhere—they were just going round and round in circles, covering the same old ground. Luke wouldn't believe her assertions that she wasn't the culprit, and the trouble was that she had nothing with which to back up her defence. There was no getting away from the fact that all the false reservations had been made in her own personal sign-in code. She'd lain awake for the last two nights, trying to think of some logical explanation for it, but the only feasible answer was one she refused to even contemplate.

She saw Luke rake an impatient hand through his thick dark hair. He was probably wishing that she were an employee so he could fire her, she thought wryly.

'Well, let's hope that this is an end to it. Presumably there's a limit to the havoc you can have wrought to Kingston Air after just one day in the Res office.'

Mike compressed her lips together and gazed stonily ahead. How could she have ever been so idiotic as to have seriously imagined that she was in danger of becoming too attracted to this arrogant, condescending, hateful male?

'But for Pete's sake, steer clear of the computers in future until you know how to use them—— Come in.' He broke off in response to the light tap at the door, and then smiled, raising his hands up in front of him. 'Sorry,' he quirked an eyebrow at Mike, 'your office.'

Still smarting from his words, Mike didn't smile back, but as her eyes rested briefly on his craggy face she was reminded all too vividly of what exactly *had* prompted those irrational fears on Friday night. Her feelings towards Luke were hardly consistent, she thought with self-disgust. One moment she was fervently wishing him at the bottom of the deepest lake, and the next moment she would look at him and the sheer force of his attraction would almost choke her. Her heart skipped a painful beat. What would it be like not to be at constant loggerheads with Luke, to feel relaxed and at ease in his company instead of perpetually on edge? Abruptly, she turned her head to greet the reservation supervisor who was approaching her desk.

'Morning,' the middle-aged woman murmured laconically and as usual came straight to the point. 'Captain Hammond says you've authorised two subload tickets for his grandchildren on this morning's Jersey.'

'That's correct,' Mike agreed. For one heartstopping moment, she'd thought she was going to be informed of yet another reservations catastrophe.

'Right. If you'd just like to sign this form, please, I'll issue the tickets.'

Mike scrawled her name with a flourish and handed it back to the supervisor, conscious all the while of the frown on Luke's face as he stood watching.

She waited until the door had closed and then looked up at him. 'Before you say anything, yes, I do know that grandchildren aren't strictly speaking eligible for concessionary travel, but I can't see that it hurts to stretch the rules slightly for once.'

'Can't you?' he enquired tightly.

'For heaven's sake, grandchildren, children, what's the difference?' She couldn't cope with any more arguments this morning.

Luke folded his arms across his chest. 'And if some other member of staff comes in tomorrow and asks you to "stretch the rules" for their auntie, second cousin, neighbour, you'll agree to that too?'

Mike frowned. 'All right, I get the point. I admit giving Captain Hammond those tickets wasn't the most sensible thing to do, but it's done now.' She paused, looking down at her desk. 'Actually,' she said candidly, 'I had my doubts at the time.'

'So why did you do it?'

Mike raised her head and as she encountered the thoughtful, perceptive grey eyes she jolted, convinced that Luke knew exactly what had prompted her to offer the discounted tickets against her better judgement. With searing shame, she acknowledged the uncomfortable truth. She'd been motivated by a childish desire to prove to the captain that she had just as much authority as Luke.

'Isn't that your telephone?' she muttered and, with relief, watched him stride towards the inner room.

The decorators had finished over the weekend and Mike had arrived at the airport on Monday to discover that Luke had vacated her office the day before and was installed in his own. At least she now had her small sanctuary back, she mused, although having a connecting door between the two rooms wasn't ideal. Luke never seemed to feel it necessary to knock before entering her domain. Depending on his mood, he either strode or sauntered in whenever he felt like doing so.

Like now, for instance. She glanced up as he stood framed in the doorway. As usual, he was wearing one of the formal dark grey suits he appeared to favour and a brilliant white shirt with a red silk tie, and she suddenly found herself wondering what he would look like in more casual clothes.

'That was Nicholas Harrison on the phone.'

'Who?' Mike murmured absently. Would Luke appear less formidable, more approachable clad in a pair of old denim jeans and a faded T-shirt?

'Nicholas Harrison,' he repeated impatiently. 'Remember him?' he added drily. 'Managing director of Link Travel, for whom Kingston Air just happen to operate charter flights to Palma and Corfu during the summer?'

'Of course I know who he is!' she returned tetchily. There was no need for him to be so sarcastic. 'I didn't happen to catch his name the first time, that's all,' she added lamely. She hadn't been paying attention, she admitted. She seemed to be suffering from these temporary lapses in concentration lately, her mind drifting off at tangents. She frowned uneasily. Surely that hadn't happened last Friday in the reservations office? No. She wasn't going to start doubting herself now, or her confidence, already severely battered, was going to be nil.

'I've asked him to have dinner with us tonight,' Luke continued casually.

'Us? Tonight?' Mike echoed. 'You might have consulted with me first to see if it was convenient! I could have been going——'

'To wash your hair?' he enquired gravely.

Mike threw him a withering look. It was like bashing her head against a brick wall!

'Why this sudden urgency to have dinner with Nicholas Harrison anyway?' she demanded, her eyes narrowing with suspicion. There was an expression on Luke's face that she didn't trust. He was up to something, she was convinced of it.

'Good PR.' He shrugged nonchalantly.

'The real reason?' Mike murmured sweetly.

He grinned. 'I bumped into Nick on Sunday night. Apparently he's considering extending his charter programme for next summer to include Crete, Tenerife and possibly Portugal.'

'Fascinating,' she retorted, her eyes fixed steadily on the craggy face. 'I hope that you made it quite clear that, while we wish him well in his new venture, Kingston Air can't possibly undertake any more charter work. We simply haven't the aircraft or crew available.' Both were stretched to the limit during the summer months.

'We could always wet lease another aircraft,' Luke answered casually, 'in which case the crew will be provided as well.'

'I'm perfectly aware of the difference between dry and wet leasing,' Mike said cuttingly.

He raised an infuriating dark eyebrow at her. 'We've obviously been studying the same textbook,' he drawled and despite herself Mike couldn't help grinning back at him. He did this to her every time, she thought ruefully—cut through her defences completely.

'Before you start listing your objections, Michaelia, all I'm suggesting is that we have dinner with Nick and discuss the idea in principle,' Luke continued. He shrugged his broad shoulders. 'Nick is doubtlessly going to negotiate with other airlines as well and see who can offer him the best overall deal.'

'But you'd like Kingston Air to get in first,' Mike said wryly. 'All right,' she sighed defeatedly. 'What time?'

'I'll pick you up at seven-thirty.'

She nodded. Seeing that Luke had to virtually pass her front door, she could hardly suggest that they drive in separate cars to the restaurant without offering a very good reason for it, she supposed. And right now her inventiveness seemed to have deserted her.

She watched him turn away and vanish behind the closed door. So much for her resolution to confine her association with him to the airport, she mused ruefully. She could always back out, even now, and claim that she'd suddenly remembered a prior engagement, but she doubted whether he would believe her. Besides, she did rather want to keep tabs on him, she admitted, and had no desire to be presented with yet another *fait accompli*. Her eyebrows furrowed together. Where exactly had Luke 'bumped into' Nicholas Harrison on Sunday evening?

As she heard the sound of a car drawing up the gravel drive outside, Mike quickly blotted her lipstick with a tissue, tucked an errant copper curl behind her ear and rose from the stool in front of the dressing-table. Picking up her evening bag from the bed, she threw a cursory glance towards the full-length mirror on the wall and frowned at the tall, slim girl with over-bright, warm hazel eyes and flushed cheeks who gazed back at her. The classically designed black dress with the demure neckline didn't seem to project the brisk, businesslike image that had been intended. The apparent severity of the style was deceptive and perversely accentuated the feminine curves it was supposed to minimise. It was too late to change now, Mike decided ruefully, glancing at her gold wristwatch, and closed the bedroom door behind her.

Automatically assuming that John would have shown him into the drawing-room, she was thrown off balance to discover Luke waiting for her at the bottom of the stairs. Faltering for a second, she continued to descend towards him, the cool casual greeting sticking in her throat as she took in his appearance, the force of his blatant, arrogant masculinity striking her like a physical blow. Expertly tailored dark trousers emphasised the lean hips and powerful thighs. His blue shirt was unbuttoned at the neck, revealing smooth tanned skin, the sprinkling of fine dark hairs becoming thicker as they disappeared down his chest.

'Ready?' The timbre of Luke's voice seemed even deeper than usual and the expression in his dark grey eyes made her heartbeat quicken.

She nodded, her throat dry, and tore her eyes away from him. The light touch of his hand on her bare arm as he guided her out of the front door and into the waiting car made her skin tingle. She gazed fixedly ahead as he started up the engine, but every nerve in her being was alive to the male presence beside her.

Slowly her erratic breathing returned to normal and she frowned as the car drew up outside a small red-bricked cottage.

'We're having dinner here?' she asked, startled, and received a confirmatory nod. She had just taken it for granted that they would be dining at a restaurant. It had never occurred to her that Luke would have elected to entertain the travel agent in the small rented cottage, although it did now explain the comparative informality of his dress.

'If you'd given me careful, detailed instructions, I'm sure I'd have managed to find my own way here,' she said drily, following him up the path to the front door. Why on earth had Luke thought it necessary to come and collect her in his car when he lived just down the lane?

She was immediately conscious of the silence as they entered the cottage. There were no sounds of activity coming from the kitchen at the far end of the narrow hall. So Luke was presumably cooking dinner himself?

Unease began to stir inside her, and grew stronger as she was shown into the living-room. Cheap reproduction prints adorned the stark white walls; the furnishings, although adequate, were well worn and ill matched. Mike's eyebrows furrowed together. This was hardly the most salubrious of settings in which to entertain a business client.

'Thank you,' she murmured coolly as Luke handed her a glass of white wine. She'd been intending to ask for a soft drink but had changed her mind at the last minute, hoping that the wine might help her relax. She sat down in an armchair and crossed her slim legs, the composed expression on her face revealing nothing of her inner disquiet, and watched Luke from under her lashes as he flicked on a table-lamp, the room instantly appearing less austere in the soft yellow glow. 'What time are you expecting Nicholas?'

'Nick?' he enquired, moving over to the sideboard and helping himself to a whisky. 'I think you're under some misapprehension, Michaelia——'

'He's not coming, is he?' Mike broke in evenly. It was a purely rhetorical question. She already knew the answer, having begun to suspect that something was amiss the moment Luke drew up in front of the cottage. 'You lied to me.'

'I never lie,' he contradicted her mildly, sitting down on the sofa and nursing the whisky tumbler in his hand.

'But you told me——'

'I told you that I'd invited Nick to dine with us tonight. Which I most certainly had.' His straight mouth quirked at the corners. 'Unfortunately he wasn't able to accept my invitation at such short notice, so we've arranged a lunchtime meeting next week.'

'You deliberately misled me!' He was simply playing with words.

'Did I?' Luke enquired with infuriating innocence.

'You know you did!' Mike took a much-needed sip of wine and surveyed him over the rim of her glass.

'So why all the subterfuge?' she demanded with a calmness she was far from feeling. 'Why didn't you simply——?'

'You might have refused again. And I hate eating alone,' he informed her gravely.

'Besides which you felt honour bound to return my lavish hospitality of the other evening?' Mike offered helpfully.

'Exactly,' he agreed, straight-faced.

'Well, thanks for the drink.' She tossed back the rest of her wine in one long gulp and rose to her feet. 'I can find my own way out.'

'You mean you're walking out on me? When I've spent hours toiling over a hot stove?'

She threw him a withering glance over her shoulder and walked briskly across to the door, but Luke was there before her and stood blocking her exit.

'Stay and have dinner with me, Mike.'

The unexpected use of the diminutive form of her name caught her off guard, while the intentness in the deep voice made her stomach muscles contract.

'Stay,' he repeated softly, and, raising a hand, gently touched her cheek with his fingers.

Mike swallowed. What did she do now? Push Luke aside and run out of the cottage like a terrified teenager? Tell him she'd stay as long as he promised not to touch her again? Either way she was going to look like an absolute fool.

'All right.' Did that cool, composed voice really belong to her? She looked up at him and her heart missed a beat as she saw the expression in his eyes as they rested lingeringly on her mouth.

'Is there anything I can do to help in the kitchen?' she asked briskly.

'You can lay the table if you like.' There was a wry note in his voice as he turned away and opened the door.

'That was delicious,' Mike murmured appreciatively as she swallowed the last morsel of tender chicken.

'My *coq au vin*——' Luke began solemnly.

'Is the toast of Paris?' Mike grinned back at him across the square table, amazed to discover that she was actually beginning to enjoy herself. They were seated in the small dining area at one end of the kitchen. There were no candles on the table, no soft, seductive music in the background. It was so far removed from the intimate dinner that she'd been dreading that her earlier agitation now seemed laughable. Luke's conversation had been light and entertaining, the sense of humour she'd once mentally accused him of lacking very much in evidence, and matching her own exactly. He had quite deliberately set out to make her feel relaxed and at ease, and he had succeeded, Mike admitted.

'And now for my *pièce de résistance*,' Luke murmured modestly, collecting the dinner plates and carrying them through to the adjoining kitchen. He stooped to open the oven door and Mike nearly choked with suppressed laughter as she witnessed the expression of dismay that crossed his face.

He stood up straight, slammed the oven door shut and grinned at her over his shoulder. 'Apparently my culinary expertise does not extend to chocolate soufflés. Cheese and fruit?'

'I don't think I could eat anything else,' Mike murmured lazily. She was almost too comfortable to move, enveloped in a rosy glow of utter well-being.

'We'll have coffee in the living-room,' Luke decided, switching on a percolator.

'OK.' Reluctantly, Mike pushed back her chair and rose to her feet. 'I'll give you a hand with the dishes first.'

'Leave them,' he instructed, setting out cups and saucers on a tray. 'I'll do them in the morning.'

'Don't you have a daily?' she asked curiously.

'No.' He shrugged. 'It hardly seems worth employing someone when I'm only going to be here temporarily.'

'I suppose not,' Mike agreed vaguely, a pang of almost unbearable sadness twisting through her. It would take a lifetime to get to know this man and she had a few short months at the very most. 'So you're fending for yourself at the moment?' she teased. 'Doing all your own laundry, shopping, cleaning as well as cooking?'

'Is there any reason why I shouldn't?' He quirked an eyebrow at her. 'Now who's being chauvinistic?'

'I was just surprised, that's all,' she defended herself quickly, remembering all too vividly their first meeting, though deliberately closing her mind to its conclusion. She wondered why Luke had decided to rent the small, rather basic cottage. Most men in his position, she was sure, would have chosen to stay in the comfort of a luxurious hotel suite. Perhaps Luke simply enjoyed being self-sufficient and living alone.

'I grew up with two strong-minded sisters who made quite sure that I didn't escape my fair share of the chores simply because I was male,' Luke explained with a smile.

Mike smiled back, intrigued by the small insight into his family background, and a childhood that had evidently not been as pampered as her own. In a house full of domestic staff, she'd never been called upon to undertake any menial chore. In fact, until she'd started her apprenticeship she'd never so much as washed a dirty mug, she realised with a pinprick of shame.

'Would you carry this through and I'll bring the coffee?' Luke handed her the tray.

She followed him back into the living-room, set the tray down carefully on the low end table in front of the sofa, and then sat down at one end.

'Cream? Sugar?' Luke asked, pouring coffee into the two cups.

'Just cream, please.'

He handed her a cup and then crossed the carpet and turned on the cassette player in one corner of the room.

'*La Traviata*,' Mike murmured, recognising the haunting, poignant music instantly. 'Prelude to Act One.' She saw Luke flick her a surprised glance and confessed, 'I don't know much about classical music or opera, but this piece was one of Matthew's favourites. He used to play it all the time.'

'You were very close, weren't you?' he said quietly, joining her on the sofa, one arm stretched out along the back behind her head.

'Yes.' She was silent for a moment. 'I hardly ever saw my father when I was a child. He was abroad a great deal of the time, and when he was home he always seemed to be rushing off to some meeting or another.' She shrugged. 'I suppose that's partly why all his marriages failed. Business always took priority over everything else.' Men like her father should never get married and have families, she thought wryly. 'But Matthew was different. However busy he was, he always made time to listen to me.' She deliberately kept her voice casual, wary of sounding over-emotional, but she could feel tears pricking the back of her eyelids. 'I know it's trite, but time really is the most precious gift you can give to a child.' She stopped, wishing she could eradicate that last remark. It sounded sentimental and banal. Cautiously she turned her head and looked up at Luke, and was instantly relieved by the deep understanding in his eyes, and she knew too that he had guessed at much that she had left unsaid, guessed at those periods of aching loneliness she'd experienced as a child in a house full of people.

'Time is the most precious commodity you can give to anyone, not just a child,' Luke murmured softly. 'And often the hardest.'

Mike was conscious that his hand had dropped to her shoulder, drawing her closer, and it suddenly seemed the most natural thing in the world to let her head fall against his chest. She could hear the strong beat of his heart, feel the warmth of his body through the thin shirt. Her eyes were on a level with the open collar, and the longing to reach out a hand and touch the tanned skin was disturbingly acute.

'Where do you come from originally?' she asked instead. She knew virtually nothing about his early life.

'North of England.'

She waited expectantly for him to elaborate on the brief, unsatisfactory answer but he made no attempt to do so. His reticence made her even more curious about his boyhood, but regretfully she decided that it might be wiser not to pursue that particular topic.

'And now you live in New York?' That was surely a safe, casual enough question.

'I divide my time between the States and Europe.'

Mike recalled Christina telling her about the apartments in New York, Geneva and Paris. Did Luke regard any of them as a home, or were they all simply strategic bases from which to conduct his business? Shades of her father, she mused ruefully. Still, at least Luke seemed to realise that marriage and a family would not fit in with his itinerant lifestyle, and contented himself with short-lived affairs. She frowned. Her only evidence for that assumption was based on the gossip columns of the more sensational tabloids, and she was already beginning to suspect that the media's portrayal of Luke was not wholly accurate. But even if his playboy image was exaggerated it was inconceivable that a man as obviously virile as Luke should be leading a celibate existence. A knot formed in the pit of her stomach. She didn't want to think about those other shadowy women in Luke's life. Not now.

Lean, sensitive fingers were stroking the nape of her neck, sending tiny little shivers tingling down her spine. She felt his lips brush against her temple, move over the curve of her cheek, and trail a sensuous, teasing path down her neck. Enclosed in a bubble of warm, languorous pleasure, she stirred against him, tilting her face upwards.

His eyes were half closed as they looked down at her, his mouth a few frustrating inches above hers. The warm, secure bubble evaporated, leaving her open and vulnerable to newer, disturbing emotions.

'Kiss me, Mike,' Luke ordered huskily.

Mike's breath lodged in her throat. Of their own volition, her hands crept up around his neck, drawing his head down towards her.

His mouth took possession of hers, gently at first and then with increasing urgency, his tongue parting her lips as he sought a deeper intimacy. Mike's eyes closed, her head spinning, tasting Luke as he was her, matching his hunger with her own, drowning in a scalding whirlpool of sensations.

His hand swept down the length of her body, and then closed possessively over her breast, his thumb stroking her nipple, already taut beneath the soft fabric of her dress. It was an exquisite form of torture, the need to feel his caress on her bare, heated skin almost unendurable.

She murmured a throaty protest as he lifted his head, her eyes opening dazedly.

'Do you have any idea of what touching you is doing to me?' he groaned, pulling her to her feet, covering her face with tiny, burning kisses as he crushed her against him, moulding her hips into the hard thrust of his thighs. Her hands gripped hold of his shoulders as she arched up against him, feverishly seeking his mouth again. She was incapable of co-herent thought; her senses, her whole being was dom-inated by this man.

She felt his hold on her relax and his arms fell to his side. The abruptness of the release left her feeling bereft and confused, her breathing shallow and ir-regular. Had she done something wrong? Uncertainly she gazed up at Luke.

'Mike, I didn't bring you here tonight to seduce you.' His voice was hoarse and strained. Gently, he stroked back a tendril of copper hair from her forehead. 'If I made love to you now—and God knows I want to—you'd never forgive me or yourself.' His eyes were dark and intent as they rested on her flushed face.

Comprehension flooded her and with it the knowledge that it would be all too easy to grow to care too much for this strong, forceful and yet unbelievably sensitive man. He could have made love to her tonight, taken advantage of her temporary insanity, and she would have been powerless to resist—wouldn't have wanted to resist, she admitted honestly. But he had taken control of the situation before it had reached its inevitable conclusion. A conclusion she most certainly would have regretted in the cold, stark light of day.

'Would you like some more coffee?'

She nodded, not trusting herself to speak, recognising that Luke had made the offer in order to give them both a few moments' breathing-space.

'I won't be long,' he murmured gruffly, picking up the empty coffee-pot and walking from the room.

Mike sat down on the sofa, curling her long legs up beside her. She concentrated all her attention on a fixed point on the white wall, trying to make her mind a complete blank, and gradually the gnawing ache inside her eased, and her pulse-rate slowed.

Her head fell back against the arm of the sofa and she stifled a yawn. She hadn't realised quite how tired she was until now, the last two sleepless nights—spent worrying about the reservation errors—taking their toll. Her eyelids began to droop downwards.

Luke was a long time fetching the coffee, Mike thought hazily. So long, in fact, that she must have dozed off waiting for him. Her eyes flickered open and she was instantly alert, aware that not only was she stretched out comfortably on the sofa but that sunlight was streaming through the windows. She hadn't simply dozed off for a few minutes—she'd spent the entire night here on Luke's sofa!

She swung her legs on to the carpet and pulled her rumpled dress over her knees, looking up as the door opened. Luke entered, with a tray, whistling loudly.

'Cup of tea?'

'I was expecting coffee,' Mike murmured drily. She glanced at her wristwatch. 'About eight hours ago.' How could anyone look and sound so impossibly cheerful at this hour of the day?

'You were fast asleep when I brought it in,' he informed her, handing her a cup and saucer. 'Come to think of it,' he added thoughtfully, 'falling asleep on me is fast becoming a habit with you.'

'I suppose it never occurred to you to wake me?' He had obviously been up for some time. He was clean shaven, his hair damp from the shower, and he had dressed in a dark suit. In contrast, she felt a wreck. Self-consciously, she ran a hand through her tousled curls. There was probably mascara smudged all around her eyes, she thought ruefully.

'I did intend to,' he murmured, moving across to an armchair with his own cup, 'once I'd had my coffee.'

'Pity to waste it once you'd made it,' Mike agreed, straight-faced. It made her feel oddly vulnerable to know that he had sat there, watching her while she slept. 'So what happened?' she prompted.

'Apparently it's catching.'

'You fell asleep, too?' she said incredulously. The way his eyes changed colour according to his moods fascinated her. When he was relaxed or amused, as now, they appeared to be blue. She drank her tea swiftly and placed the cup down on the low table. 'May I use the bathroom, please?' If she could just wash her face, she might begin to feel more human.

'Upstairs. Last door on the left,' Luke informed her laconically.

She mounted the narrow wooden staircase and made her way along the tiny landing. One of the bedroom doors was open and she couldn't resist the temptation to glance in, the male paraphernalia strewn about indicating that it was the room Luke was currently occupying. Her eyes were drawn to the large double bed by the window. What would it have felt like to have woken up this morning in that bed, with Luke lying beside her, his arms around her? The mental images that thought conjured up made her face burn, and she hurried towards the bathroom.

It was much as she'd expected: old-fashioned, but spotlessly clean. She ran piping hot water into the white porcelain basin and studied herself briefly in the mirror hanging above it. She didn't look quite as dishevelled as she'd feared. In fact, considering she'd spent the night fully dressed on a sofa, she looked amazingly fresh and wide awake.

Returning downstairs, she discovered Luke in the kitchen, tending a frying-pan on the stove.

'Egg and bacon? Or just toast and coffee?' He glanced at her over his shoulder.

'I'd prefer to go straight home.' She longed for a bath and a change of clothes.

'After you've spent the night with me, the least I can do is cook you breakfast,' he drawled, his mouth quirking at the corners.

'Standard practice?' she enquired sweetly. The aroma of sizzling bacon was beginning to make her mouth water. 'All right.' She changed her mind. 'I'll stay.' The bath could wait for another twenty minutes.

At her request, Luke dropped her off at the end of the long drive leading up to Rakers' Moon.

'Thanks.' She smiled, her hand on the door-handle, and was taken completely by surprise as he leant over and kissed her firmly on the mouth.

'See you at the airport,' he murmured softly.

She watched him drive away and began to meander up the drive. A rabbit darted across in front of her and disappeared through the hedge into the field beyond. She paused and took a deep breath, gazing up at the cloudless azure sky. A perfect spring morning, she thought with a rush of quite ridiculous happiness. She began to walk more briskly towards the house and then couldn't resist breaking into a jog, exhilaration and energy sweeping through her.

The mood of near euphoria was still with her when she arrived at the airport. She walked through the passenger terminal, trying to look brisk and purposeful, but her mouth kept curving into an idiotic smile.

The connecting door was open as she entered her office and for a moment she stood motionless, gazing unobserved at Luke as he sat with his dark head bowed over the paperwork strewn across his desk.

'Luke?' she addressed him softly, her eyes glowing as they moved over the rugged, male features.

Abruptly, he lifted his head, and she felt as if she'd been doused with icy water as she met the chilling grey gaze.

CHAPTER SIX

MIKE stared numbly back at Luke, unable to believe that this cold, forbidding stranger was the same man with whom she'd shared a light-hearted, companionable breakfast little more than an hour ago. How could anyone change quite so dramatically in such a short space of time?

'I suppose there's been another reservation error.' She finally found her voice.

'You've really excelled yourself this time, Michaelia,' he grated.

He pushed back his chair noisily, and strode towards her, thrusting a piece of paper into her hand which she quickly identified as a reservations computer printout. She gave it a quick, cursory glance and blanched as she saw the name of the passengers at the top of the amended itinerary.

'Mr and Mrs N. Harrison. Nicholas Harrison?' she said weakly.

'None other,' he told her grimly. 'It's Nick's wife birthday today and he'd arranged a surprise day-trip to Paris. Needless to say he wasn't exactly amused to discover that his reservation had been cancelled.' Luke's face looked as if it had been carved out of hard, unyielding rock. 'It hardly augurs well for our meeting with him next week, does it?'

Mike faced him squarely. Was he expecting her to humbly apologise—for something she knew full well she hadn't been guilty of?

'Luke,' she began steadily, 'I don't know what's been happening exactly, but I didn't——'

'For Pete's sake, don't start denying it again,' he cut in tersely.

'But——'

'Just drop it, will you?' He turned on his heel and strode back into his office, slamming the connecting door shut behind him.

Mike walked over to her chair and sat down, drumming her fingers on the desk top. She felt so frustrated she could scream! This must be exactly how someone accused of a crime they hadn't commited must feel. Luke wouldn't even listen to her, let alone believe her assertion that she was not responsible for the continuing reservation errors.

Her mouth curved wryly. What an idiot she was! She'd been misguided enough to think that Luke was beginning to like and respect her. His restraint last night had seemed to indicate that he cared enough about her not to want to hurt her. Her lips compressed together in a tight line. And now he was practically accusing her of being a liar—or at least doubting her word, which virtually amounted to the same thing.

Sighing, she began to examine the copy of Nicholas Harrison's booking again, and then stiffened, elation and hope sweeping over her. Here it was, in black and white, the proof she so desperately needed. Not even Luke could argue with this concrete evidence of her innocence.

She leapt to her feet and marched across to the connecting door, flinging it open.

'Don't say a word!' she said shortly as Luke lifted his head impatiently. She tossed the piece of paper down on his desk. 'Read through that again.'

'Michaelia, I have a heavy workload ahead of me today, and am in no mood to play games,' he said testily.

'Look at the last line,' she ordered, eyes glinting.

His eyes flickered down the page. 'Your reference and the date on which you cancelled the booking.' He frowned, and as he looked up Mike saw the growing comprehension in his eyes. 'Last Sunday's date.'

'When I wasn't anywhere near the airport, let alone in the res office,' she finished triumphantly.

'You realise what this means, don't you?' Luke said slowly. 'Someone has quite deliberately been using your personal sign in code to falsify reservation entries in the computer.'

She nodded, goose-pimples crawling over her flesh. The knowledge that a member of the Kingston Air staff had intentionally set out to discredit her made her feel slightly sick. Who would want to be that vindictive, and why?

'You suspected this right from the start, didn't you?' Luke asked abruptly and saw the confirmation on her face. 'Why the hell didn't you tell me sooner, instead of letting it drag on this long?'

Mike gazed at him incredulously. He was beyond belief! Not only had he so far failed to apologise for misjudging her, but he was now blaming her for not reporting her suspicions to him sooner. What did he think she'd been trying to do ever since the first error came to light?

'Other than you and I, who has a list of the staff computer codes?' he demanded, his mind leaping ahead.

'The res supervisor of course.' She paused. 'And . . . Andrew Simpson,' she admitted reluctantly. Her eyes met the grey ones. 'It can't be Andrew,' she protested weakly. 'I know he was angry and upset on Friday after the staff meeting, but surely he wouldn't...? I mean, he'd be hurting the airline, not just me. Besides,' she continued more firmly, 'I had lunch with him in the canteen on Saturday when you were in London, and he seemed perfectly happy and relaxed.' He'd spent most of the time talking about the past, Mike recalled with a twinge of unease.

'Andrew had the opportunity,' Luke said quietly. 'He was on late shift on Friday and Sunday and was probably the last to leave the office on both occasions.'

'This is all pure speculation. We've no real proof.' And they were never likely to have, Mike thought, unless they caught the culprit red-handed—and that was a very remote possibility. 'Surely the most sensible thing to do would be to simply change my code?' She should have confided in the reservation supervisor and done that immediately, she realised belatedly.

'I think we should talk to Andrew.'

'And accuse him outright?' Mike said, horrified.

'Credit me with a little more subtlety than that,' Luke answered drily and glanced towards the door. 'Come in.'

Tina entered carrying coffee and biscuits and set them down on the desk. With mild amusement, Mike noticed that, while she had been given the standard staff mug, Luke had a china cup and saucer.

'Chocolate wafers,' Luke murmured appreciatively and smiled up at the receptionist, who immediately turned scarlet with gratification. 'Would you ask Andrew to come to my office when it's convenient? Thank you, Tina.'

'I only ever get digestives,' Mike observed drily as Tina departed.

'I think I should talk to Andrew alone.' Luke sat back in his chair, and surveyed her with dark, inscrutable eyes.

'No,' she protested. 'This concerns me more than anyone.'

'As you wish. But for heaven's sake, sit down. Relax. Have a biscuit.'

Reluctantly, Mike positioned herself on a hard-backed chair. She started to reach for a chocolate biscuit and then changed her mind. It would probably choke her right now, and she watched in silent amazement as Luke, rather absently, cleared the plate. She would never have suspected him of having a sweet tooth. Perhaps he was just addicted to chocolate, she mused, her eyes softening as she recalled the failed soufflé.

She tensed as she heard the sound of approaching footsteps and looked up to see Andrew standing in the open doorway.

'You wanted to see me?'

'Come in and sit down,' Luke said courteously, indicating the chair drawn up in front of his desk. He waited until Andrew was seated before continuing, 'As you know, there's been a spate of reservation errors this week.'

'I *should* know,' Andrew broke in calmly, 'seeing that I was responsible for them.' There was a glint of triumph in his eyes as they swept over Mike's shocked, stunned face, and then abruptly he threw back his head and started to laugh.

The high-pitched, brittle, unearthly sound seemed to vibrate right through Mike's body. For a moment she couldn't move, her legs paralysed, couldn't think, her mind numb, and then, as if she were in a trance, she rose to her feet and approached Andrew.

'I don't understand,' she muttered hoarsely. 'Why, Andrew? What was the point...?' Her words stuck in her throat as she saw the almost manic glow in his eyes. My God, this man hated her!

'I've worked for KA for twenty years,' he turned on her savagely. 'I've helped to build it up into the success it is today.' His voice rose with his mounting fury. 'Kingston Air should be mine now by rights.' His lips curled contemptuously. 'And instead Matthew left it to a pampered, spoilt little bitch like you. Did you seriously imagine for one moment that I'd be prepared to go on working for you, for a...?' A torrent of vile obscenities poured from his mouth.

Mike tried to block them out but they crawled into her flesh like maggots. She saw Luke half rise to his feet, his hands clenched into fists, and for one awful moment thought that he was going to strike Andrew, and then instinctively she knew that he would never resort to physical violence, and most certainly not against a man so much older than himself.

She slumped back on to her chair before her legs gave way and, as if from a great distance, she heard a cold, authoritative voice snapping out words. They seemed to have the desired effect because Andrew fell silent. Then, with increasing horror, she saw that he had started to cry, tears coursing down his lined, weather-beaten cheeks.

He suddenly looked so old and pathetic that Mike's heart twisted. It was unbearable to watch him. She desperately wanted to go over and comfort him but she was probably the last person in the world he would want anywhere near him. His outburst had sickened her, shaken her to the core, but somehow sitting here now, witnessing his distress and being powerless to help, was infinitely more shocking and upsetting.

'What's going to happen to me now?' Andrew finally spoke, his voice wavering.

Mike looked across at Luke, silently imploring him to deal gently with this pitiful, clearly unbalanced elderly man. Then, as she saw that deep compassion had replaced the blazing anger n the grey eyes, she knew that her fears had been unwarranted. How could she have ever supposed Luke to be utterly ruthless and insensitive? she thought wonderingly. Her gaze swept over his familiar face. *I love him*. Of all the times for her subconscious mind to drop that little bombshell, she thought with mounting hysteria. How could she possibly love a man she had known for such a short space of time? She was overwrought, her emotions confused and unreliable. It couldn't be true. She refused to accept it.

'Early retirement,' Luke said quietly. 'On a full pension.'

Andrew nodded, looking utterly defeated. 'Do you want me to leave the airport straight away, now?'

'I think it would be best.'

The grey-haired man rose silently to his feet.

'Andrew!' Mike blurted out his name, moving towards him. She had to say something to him, couldn't simply let him walk out like this after twenty years with the airline.

He gazed back at her, his eyes curiously vacant, and then, with great deliberation, wordlessly turned his back on her and walked out of the office.

'Here, have this.'

Mike hadn't even been aware that she was crying, until Luke pressed a white handkerchief into her icy hand. Rather ineffectually, she dabbed at her eyes, trying to stem the hot, salty tears.

'I had no idea that Andrew resented me so much.' She tried to keep her voice steady, but it came out in a strangled sob.

'It's all right, Mike.' Luke drew her into the circle of his arms, and began to stroke her hair, soothing her as if she were a child.

'I've known him since I was a baby,' she mumbled into his shoulder. 'And all the time . . . he hated me.' She swallowed. 'Matthew should have given him at least some shares. He had far more right to them than I,' she said fiercely. 'Oh, Luke, he looked so old and vulnerable.' Her voice broke again.

'There's something I ought to tell you,' he said quietly, his chin resting on top of her head. 'I should probably have told you before now,' he admitted. 'Shortly after I became involved with Kingston Air, I started to receive a succession of letters from Andrew.' His mouth tightened. 'They could loosely be termed poison-pen letters, except that they weren't anonymous, and the venom wasn't directed at me but at Matthew.'

Mike lifted her head from his shoulder, wondering how many more shocks she could deal with today. 'What did they say?' she asked miserably.

'The gist of them was that Andrew felt it was his duty to inform me that Matthew was becoming increasingly senile and was no longer capable of running the airline.'

'I don't believe it!' Mike's eyes darkened incredulously. 'Did you tell Matthew?'

'I didn't have much alternative.'

'He must have felt so betrayed and hurt,' she said slowly, hardly able to bear the thought.

'Yes, I'm sure he did,' Luke agreed. 'But he was just like you.' He touched the side of her face with his hand. 'He had a strong, if in my view misguided sense of loyalty, and he refused to take any action against Andrew as long as he remained competent at his job. Andrew has been mentally unbalanced for a long time now. In no circumstances would Matthew have given him any shares in the company.'

'Is that why you wanted to fire Andrew that first day?'

'I thought it would save us both a lot of trouble in the long run, but you refused quite adamantly to dismiss him.' He shrugged. 'That's partly why I decided to come down to the airport for a while, so that I could keep an eye on him.'

'And partly because you thought I was incapable of running the airline myself?' Mike queried, stiffening.

'I shouldn't have phrased it quite like that, but, yes, if you want the truth, I didn't think you had sufficient experience. And I still don't,' he added candidly. 'Not yet.'

'I see.' Mike eased herself from his arms and started to turn away, but Luke caught hold of her hands and swung her around in front of him.

'Don't be so touchy,' he mocked gently. 'I can just imagine your reaction if I announced that I was going to do a quick wheel-change on November Echo.'

'I'd warn the air crew!' She grinned reluctantly, acknowledging the point he was making, but his teasing comment did little to fill that cold void deep inside her. She felt emotionally drained, and utterly defeated. Did all the staff secretly resent her as much as did Andrew, consider her as incompetent as did Luke?

'I could never understand why Matthew sold half his shares to you,' she said quietly. 'But now I do.'

Even her beloved grandfather hadn't had complete faith in her ability to run Kingston Air on her own. Taking on Luke as his partner had been his insurance policy for the future.

She crossed the office floor and stood with her back to Luke, gazing out of the window. 'If you still want to buy me out, you can,' she said dully. 'I really don't care any more.' Slowly, she turned around to face him, and the anger in the dark grey eyes made her flinch.

'I thought you were a fighter! And now, at the first sign of trouble, you want to throw the towel in, and wallow in self-pity!'

The scorn and contempt in his voice cut right through her. Frozen-faced, she headed for the door, desperately needing to be alone, to be as far away from both Luke and the airport as possible.

Jeans-clad legs stretched out in front of her, Mike sat on the grass by the dew pond, her turbulent thoughts out of harmony with the tranquil, peaceful setting.

Dispiritedly, she picked up a pebble and tossed it into the still, translucent green water, watching the ripples spread outwards to the edge of the pond. She felt such an idiot. This was the second time in just over a week that she'd fled from the airport like an over-sensitive, slightly neurotic adolescent. How Luke must be despising her right now, she thought, squirming inwardly.

She was fully aware that she didn't as yet have the necessary expertise to run Kingston Air, had admitted that long ago, so why had she felt so hurt simply because Luke had endorsed that view? Her reaction had been illogical and completely irrational. Worst of all, what had possessed her to offer him her shares? It had been a futile, fatuous gesture, because she had no real intention of parting with them.

Or had she? If she severed all connections with Kingston Air, she would also be cutting off her link with Luke. He would be out of her life for good. But was that what she really wanted, never to see Luke again?

What was the matter with her? she wondered desperately. In the past she'd always been so rational and level-headed, had always been so sure of how she felt and what she wanted, but ever since she'd encountered Luke she seemed to be in an uncharacteristic state of perpetual confusion and uncertainty.

Did she love him? Last night she had wanted him to make love to her but that was hardly the same thing. Wasn't it simply that some puritanic part of her had been secretly appalled by the strength of her response to him last night, had refused to acknowledge that it had been purely a physical one, preferring to couch it in more acceptable terms?

She sighed. This self-analysis was utterly pointless. She was running away from the truth, exactly as she had run away from the airport. Against her better judgement, despite her steadfast belief that it wasn't possible to fall in love with a man she had known for barely a month, she had done exactly that.

She started as she felt a hand touch her shoulder and turned her head rapidly.

'Luke!' She scrambled to her feet, totally disconcerted by his unexpected appearance. It was as if she had miraculously managed to conjure him up out of her thoughts. He was also the very last person she wanted to see now, just when she was trying to come to terms with her new, quite horrific discovery. 'How did you know I was here?'

'I've been up to the house and John told me that you'd gone for a walk and suggested that I might find you here.'

'I used to come here a lot when I was a child. John must have remembered.' It was appropriate that she had chosen one of her childhood haunts today, she thought wryly, considering her juvenile behaviour. 'I used to bring my bucket and spade with me and dig round the edge of the pond, convinced I was going to find some long-forgotten contraband.' Seeing his look of incomprehension, she started to tell him about the smuggling connection. She was conscious that she was talking too much but she couldn't seem to stop. Perhaps she was one of those people who chattered unceasingly when they were nervous. She had no experience to draw on for that supposition, because she'd never before felt so edgy in someone else's presence. Was this what love did to you, reduced you to a gibbering wreck? If that was the case, she wanted no part of it, would fight it every inch of the way. She loathed this sensation of no longer being in total command of herself. If only Luke would say something, she might feel less agitated, but he just stood there in silence, watching her, his eyes narrowed against the bright glare of the sun.

'Would you like a coffee?' she asked weakly, indicating the Thermos flask at her feet, determined to evoke some response from him.

'No, thanks.' He took a step towards her and placed his hands on her shoulders, so that she had to tilt her head to look up at him.

'Mike, I'm sorry,' he said abruptly. 'I shouldn't have been so tough on you earlier, not after what you'd just gone through with Andrew.'

Andrew. Did love make you self-centred, as well? She hadn't even thought about Andrew and that appalling scene since she'd left the airport. Her mind had been dominated by the man who was now standing far too close for comfort. Already her body was instinctively responding to his proximity, her heartbeat quickening, her stomach dipping as if she were on a roller-coaster.

'I thought you'd come back at me, guns blazing,' Luke continued with a wry smile. 'I never anticipated that you'd just walk out on me like that.' Gently he touched the side of her face. 'Truce?'

Mike schooled her features into what she fervently hoped would pass for a casual smile of agreement.

'Good,' he murmured quietly and then, giving her no warning, bent his head and kissed her with a fierce hunger that left her trembling and breathless.

'I've wanted to do that since the moment you walked into the office this morning,' he muttered thickly.

'And instead you——' Her words were drowned as his mouth came down on hers again, his hand moving to her hip, drawing her body against him. Fighting against that swirling pleasure before it engulfed her completely, Mike pressed her hands against his chest, pushing him away from her.

'What's the matter, Mike?' He frowned, his breathing as unsteady as her own.

'We have to work together, see each other every day at the airport,' she said shakily. 'I just don't think it's a good idea to become...involved in any way.'

For one awful moment, she dreaded that he was going to laugh at her, tell her that a few kisses didn't constitute his idea of a relationship, but he didn't. His eyes were dark and unreadable, but definitely not amused.

'Normally, I'd agree with you,' he said quietly, 'but, as I'm only going to be at the airport for such a short time, I think we could make an exception for once, don't you?'

'So I'm just going to be a temporary diversion before you fly back to New York or wherever else your business takes you,' Mike muttered, her voice brittle, stabbing pain tearing through her.

'That is an insult—to both of us,' Luke rasped.

Her eyes, locked into his, saw the anger in the dark grey depths. Already she was bitterly regretting her remark, no longer sure of its veracity.

'I'm sorry,' she mumbled. Luke would never deliberately set out to use or hurt anyone, she thought with sudden conviction.

'Come on,' he said gruffly. 'I'll drive you home. My car's in the lane.'

'It'll only take me fifteen minutes to walk back through the fields,' she started to protest and then changed her mind. She ought to go back to work at the airport, she supposed. Tempting though it was, she could hardly spend the rest of the day sitting here in the sun, aimlessly tossing pebbles into the pond.

Retrieving the flask and the blue and white sweatshirt which she'd earlier discarded, she followed Luke through the small copse of trees to the waiting car.

She slipped in beside him, clicked on her seatbelt, and then frowned as the car moved off smoothly. 'This is the wrong way. Rakers' is in the other direction.'

'I know.'

'You said you'd give me a lift home.' She was suddenly intensely suspicious of the expression on his face. He looked far too nonchalant.

'I intend to.' He paused. 'Eventually.'

'You may not tell lies, Luke Duncan, but you certainly stretch the truth,' Mike informed him with mock severity. 'So what little surprise do you have in store for me now?' she asked lightly.

'I decided that it was about time I saw something of Dorset,' he announced calmly. 'And I've nominated you as my guide.' He gave a quick sideways grin. 'I'm completely in your hands, Mike. Yours to command. All I ask is that you be gentle with me.'

Mike's heart flipped over as she met his teasing gaze in the driving-mirror. Oh, God, she loved him so much it hurt. 'What about that heavy workload?'

'It'll keep. Right, where to first?'

A burst of pure, undiluted happiness swept through her. She didn't care about the future, not even tomorrow. All that mattered was here and now. And being with Luke.

The day had passed far too quickly, Mike thought sadly, her eyes resting on Luke, the breeze ruffling his dark hair as he sat by her side, gazing out across Swanage Bay. Far below them waves crashed against the rocky coastline.

'What are they called?' he asked, indicating the curiously shaped weathered rocks jutting out from the headland.

'Old Harry Rocks.' She shivered and untied the sweatshirt draped around her shoulders and tugged it over her head. The sun's rays were weakening, reminding her that the warmth of the day had been deceptive, that it was still only April.

'You're getting cold.' The concern in Luke's voice made her feel cherished and cared for. 'We'd better be getting back, I suppose.' She was inordinately pleased to hear the note of regret in his voice and wondered if he was as reluctant as she for this stolen day to end.

He helped her to her feet and then instead of releasing her hand kept it firmly enclosed in his. Blissfully conscious of the warm, strong fingers against her palm, Mike walked in contented silence by Luke's side as they retraced their steps along the cliff path to the car.

They stopped at Corfe Castle on their homeward journey, the picturesque village dominated by the castle ruins situated at the top of a conical hill.

'Race you to the top,' Luke challenged.

'You're on,' Mike responded laughingly, and broke into a sprint, but, to her chagrin, he quickly passed her.

'Warmer now?' he greeted her teasingly as she arrived at the top, several minutes after him. Before she had time to catch her breath, he drew her into his arms and kissed her lingeringly on the mouth.

'Did you know the sun's brought out even more tiny little freckles on your nose?' he murmured huskily, lifting his head and gently tracing the contour of her face with his finger.

'Has it?' Mike said weakly, looking at him with dazed eyes, hoping that he would attribute her rapid breathing to her recent exertion.

Keeping an arm around her shoulders, Luke surveyed the panoramic view below them.

'I spend so little time in England these days that I tend to forget just how beautiful the countryside is.'

Mike's stomach lurched and she averted her eyes from Luke's face. If he had deliberately set out to destroy her happiness he couldn't have done so more effectively.

Today had been an illusion, like the fake summer weather. Nothing more. For a few hours she'd been living in a fool's paradise, but Luke's casual remark had forced her back to harsh reality with a jolt, reminding her of just how transitory was his presence both in England and in her life. Whatever happened, she must not allow him to become too important to her, she told herself fiercely, and then, with a feeling of sick inevitability, knew that it was already too late.

The setting sun painted the sky crimson as the car turned into the drive leading up to Rakers' Moon. If Mike had been unnaturally subdued on the journey back, Luke hadn't appeared to notice, had himself lapsed into silence, seemingly totally preoccupied with his own thoughts.

'Hungry?' He turned to her with a smile as he drew up in front of the house. 'I'll book a table at the Smuggler's Rest for eight-thirty.' He glanced at his wristwatch. 'That should give us both time to shower and change.' He paused, seeing the expression on her face. 'I'm taking rather a lot for granted, aren't I?' he said quietly. 'Would you do me the honour of dining with me tonight, Miss Harrington?' he asked with mock formality, his eyes teasing her.

Mike hesitated. She ought to tell him right now that she didn't want their relationship to progress any further, wanted it to return to a safe, businesslike footing. But was it possible to turn the clock back, wipe out last night and today as if they had never happened?

'Luke, I don't——' she began uncertainly and then her words were drowned as he bent his head and kissed her gently but expertly on the mouth. How was she supposed to make a rational decision when she couldn't even think straight? Mike thought despairingly, every nerve-ending in her body tingling.

'I'll pick you up in forty minutes.'

'All right,' she agreed weakly.

She watched him drive away and, closing the front door, leaned against it and took a deep, controlling breath. Why shouldn't she grab what happiness she could while Luke was still at the airport? Whatever she chose to do now, the end result was going to be the same anyway, so why didn't she simply live each day as it came, and postpone the inevitable hurt and pain for as long as possible? Eyes cloudy with irresolution, she mounted the stairs.

Clad in a peach satin dressing-gown, her skin delicately scented with expensive soap, Mike emerged from the bathroom. Rubbing her damp hair with a white towel, she opened the door of her wardrobe and inspected the contents, wishing that she'd brought a wider selection of clothes with her from London. She'd wear the green silk, she decided, having been initially attracted to the dress because of its rich, vibrant colour. Turning round, she caught a glimpse of her reflection in the mirror and grinned back mockingly. With those wide, apprehensive hazel eyes, she looked as nervous as a teenager on her first date, she thought wryly.

The telephone on her bedside table summoned her attention and she walked swiftly across the carpet and picked up the receiver.

'Luke Duncan, Miss Harrington.'

'Thank you, John. Would you put him through, please?'

She heard the sound of the downstairs telephone being replaced and sat down comfortably on the edge of the bed.

'Mike?'

Just hearing the sound of the familiar, deep voice was enough to send a tremor through her body.

'I'm afraid I'm going to have to cancel dinner tonight . . . Mike, are you still there?'

'Yes, of course,' she responded lightly, forcing the acute disappointment from her voice.

'My Geneva office has been trying to get hold of me all day,' he continued briskly. 'I'm going straight out there tonight.'

'Geneva? Tonight?' she echoed in disbelief. Surely whatever it was that needed his attention could wait until the morning? 'Isn't it too late to catch the last flight from Heathrow?'

'I've arranged for the company jet to pick me up down here. In fact it should be airborne and on its way any minute.' There was a pause at the other end of the line. 'Mike, I really am sorry. I wouldn't be going if it weren't absolutely necessary.'

How many times had she heard those exact words being uttered insincerely by her father during her childhood? He'd used them on the countless occasions he'd failed to honour his promise to attend her birthday parties, or open day at school, or when he'd postponed some eagerly awaited outing.

'I'll be quite glad to have an early night, actually,' she heard a voice, presumably her own, murmur casually. 'Have a good trip.'

'I should be back tomorrow evening, all being well. Goodnight, Mike.'

She replaced the receiver and then flung herself back across her bed and stared bleakly at the ceiling. Luke was just like her father, she thought drearily. In the final analysis, his business commitments would always take priority over everything else.

CHAPTER SEVEN

'THANK you, Mr Evans. We'll be in touch in a few days to let you know our decision.'

The tall, pleasant-faced man rose from his chair, murmured a courteous farewell, and departed from the office.

Luke pushed back his chair, stretched his arms above his head and looked wearily at Mike. 'Well?'

'He certainly seems very qualified for the post,' she said reluctantly.

'But?' Luke bit out the word. 'What's wrong this time? Let me guess. You don't trust men with brown eyes, his feet are too large, you didn't like the colour of his tie?'

She flushed, her fingers flicking the edge of the folder laid out on the desk in front of her. This was the ninth candidate they'd interviewed for the position of manager over the past few days, and so far she'd raised objections to each one.

'I just wondered if perhaps he was a little too old...I mean, he's only recently taken early retirement from his last job——'

'And soon realised that he'd made a mistake,' Luke interrupted impatiently. 'What's the matter with you, Mike? This is beginning to verge on the farcical.'

'I don't think we should rush into anything, that's all,' she said lamely.

'I hardly think it's "rushing into things" to employ someone of Steven Evans's calibre. In fact, we're damn lucky to get him and if we don't move quickly someone else is going to snap him up.'

'You're right,' she agreed unhappily. 'He's ideal.'

'And it's an added bonus that he'll be able to start virtually straight away.'

'I suppose it is,' she mumbled, thinking the exact reverse.

Luke rose to his feet in a swift, controlled movement. 'I'm going to see what's happening in Ops.'

'Do you seriously think we're going to have some diversions?' she asked as he walked to the outer door.

'I should say there's a strong possibility if the weather doesn't improve at Gatwick and Heathrow, and it remains clear here.'

Mike leaned back in her chair and sighed heavily as Luke closed the door behind him. She'd hoped that it would take months to find a suitable replacement for Andrew, not merely three weeks. With the installation of a new, competent, experienced manager, it wouldn't be long before Luke decided that his own presence at the airport was unnecessary.

He would probably be relieved to go, she thought with a painful twist of her heart. Not only did his interest in her appear to have waned, but she was beginning to suspect that he was becoming increasingly bored with Kingston Air now that it was operating so smoothly, the airline's transition to handling agent having been completed without a hitch last week.

Mereton Holdings was demanding more and more of his attention. The company executive jet was now based on permanent standby at the airport and Luke made frequent trips abroad, as well as up to London, compensating for his absence on his return by working late into the night at the airport.

Other than for a couple of business lunches, she hadn't once seen Luke outside the airport since the day they'd spent exploring Dorset together. There had been no more invitations to dinner, no more shared expeditions to the coast.

All her heart-searching had been for nothing. There was no need to make any decision about her relationship with Luke—because it was now non-existent. Mereton Holdings and Kingston Air between them monopolised his every waking hour. He simply no longer had time left for her.

Sometimes, he seemed so preoccupied that she doubted he was even aware of her existence, despite her physical proximity. At other times, some sixth sense would alert her to his presence, and she would turn her head and discover him standing in the open doorway of his office, watching her with dark, inscrutable eyes, but whether he was thinking about her, or she just happened to be in his line of vision, she had no idea.

She missed him acutely on the days he was absent from the airport, and yet when he was there she felt tense and on edge. Occasionally he would casually, almost absent-mindedly, invite her to lunch in the staff canteen, but she always refused the invitations on some pretext or other, wary that in a less formal setting she might inadvertently betray herself. It was vital that he should never suspect the strength of her feelings for him, not simply through pride but because it would make the situation at work even more unbearable than it was already.

She, too, was putting in long hours at the airport, her administrative knowledge and skills improving daily, and she usually returned to Rakers' Moon in the late evening, too tired to do anything but eat a solitary supper and tumble into bed. Then invariably, as tired as she was, her sleep would be disturbed by images of Luke, and she would finally fall into a restless slumber just before dawn, to be woken shortly afterwards by the insistent clamour of her alarm clock.

Unenthusiastically, Mike selected a folder at random from her in-tray. She hadn't appreciated until the past few weeks just how much mundane, tedious paperwork was involved in running the small airline, and was finding it increasingly irksome to be stuck behind a desk for most of the day. Sometimes she gave in to temptation, and escaped from the confines of her office and went for a brisk walk around the airport to clear her mind, always drawn in the end towards the engineering section. She missed her old job, she thought ruefully, and was beginning to have grave doubts about her aptitude for administration.

She glanced up as the outer door was flung open.

'Gatwick's clamped in fog. Visibility at Heathrow is just on limits and trending downwards,' Luke announced laconically and then grinned. 'First diversion, Corfu en route to Gatwick, expected in twenty minutes.'

Mike pushed back her chair, her eyes brightening with anticipation. This was more like it, she thought with elation, slamming the folder shut.

'The paperwork of Victor Uniform, the 737 from Malaga,' Mike murmured, edging her way through the crowded operations-room to where Luke was seated opposite the senior duty officer.

'Thanks.' Luke took the large envelope from her hand and deposited it in a tray with the outer aircraft documentation awaiting his attention. 'Anne...' he glanced over his shoulder '...would you go down to the Customs hall, please, and see how Jackie's coping? Tell her the end is in sight,' he added with a quick smile. 'Sue, the passengers for the outbound Palma should be arriving by coach any minute now. They've all been checked in and issued with boarding cards at Gatwick, so you can take them straight through Security and Immigration.'

Both girls immediately replaced their uniform hats and gloves and headed for the door.

Mike perched on the edge of an empty desk, resting her throbbing feet, and surveyed the exhausted faces around her. Some of the staff had been on duty since half-past five this morning and it was now nearly nine o'clock at night, and yet not one of them had complained. They'd worked tirelessly through the day with virtually no break; and it was only now that the pressure had eased that their weariness was starting to show.

There was a knock at the office door and, as she was nearest, Mike went to answer it, slightly taken aback to find herself confronted by a large, overalled man clutching a number of cardboard containers.

'I was told to come straight through,' he announced. 'Pizzas.'

'Right, thank you.' Luke came up behind her and collected the boxes, fishing in his pocket for some money. He looked around at the assembled staff. 'Hope you all like pizzas,' he smiled. 'Now take them through to the crew-room and then go home,' he ordered. 'You too,' he added, turning to the senior duty officer. 'I'll see the Palma out.' He paused and added quietly, 'And thanks.'

'What about the inbound Guernsey?' someone asked immediately.

'I'll stay on and meet that,' Mike said swiftly, her eyes resting on Luke's dark head. He had been in his element today, she thought, her mouth curving softly, his enthusiasm affecting every single member of the staff. Even now, as exhausted as they were, they were reluctant to go home.

In addition to their own schedule and charter services Kingston Air handled twenty-nine flights diverted from Gatwick and Heathrow. Some of the aircraft had night stopped and would be positioned back to their base airport in the morning. Others had departed for a variety of European destinations with a fresh crew on board, and passengers transported down from London.

Without Luke's cool, calm leadership, his skills as a co-ordinator, Mike had no doubts that the day would have dissolved into complete pandemonium. It had still been chaotic, she thought with an inward smile— but an organised chaos.

The sudden influx of nearly three thousand extra passengers into the small, provincial airport had placed a severe strain on all its facilities. The arrivals lounges hadn't been designed to cater for such numbers, and on occasions there had been no option other than to keep passengers waiting on board their aircraft until the congestion in the over-crowded lounges eased. The unavoidable delay had inevitably caused some passengers to become irritable and bad-tempered, but, Mike remembered with a rush of pride, every one of the airline staff had remained cool and calm, had dealt with even the most abusive of passengers with unfailing courtesy and patience—only letting off steam when they had returned to the operations-room.

The two girls returned from the Customs hall, announcing that the last coachload of passengers had departed for London, and Luke dispatched them to join the others in the crew-room.

'I'll go and see the Palma off,' he murmured to Mike, picking up the paperwork, 'if you'd like to listen out for the Guernsey.' He paused on his way to the door and studied her tired, drawn face. 'You look exhausted,' he said quietly.

'I am,' she admitted, the concern on his face making her stomach dip, 'but it's been worth it.' Hazel eyes locked into grey ones and simultaneously they both started to grin.

'We did it!' Luke grabbed hold of her hands and swung her around in front of him, the use of the plural warming her as much as the pressure of his fingers. He looked and sounded as elated as if he'd just completed a multimillion pound boardroom deal, Mike thought, feeling closer to him than she had for weeks, loving him so much that it was a physical pain.

His face sobered and slowly he drew her towards him, his eyes holding hers.

'Mike...' His hands threaded through her silky curls, tilting her head upwards and his mouth, warm, firm and sensual, took possession of hers.

There was no steady rise of languorous pleasure but an explosion of senses as all Mike's pent-up longing of days was released. Her lips parted under the urgent demands of his mouth, her hands reached up and clung to the hard, muscular shoulders. The blood roared in her ears. She was spinning out of control, oblivious to everything but that driving ache deep inside her, that desperation to be even closer to Luke.

'Alpha November to Kingston Air.'

She heard Luke's sharp intake of breath as he lifted his head and looked towards the radio, his eyes dark and disorientated as if he, like her, was having difficulty in recalling his surroundings.

'I'll answer it,' Mike said shakily. 'The Palma...' she reminded him.

He nodded wordlessly, abruptly stooped down to retrieve the papers scattered on the floor at their feet, and then strode out of the office.

Taking a deep, controlling breath, Mike moved across the room to the radio, her responses automatic, and then slumped weakly down on to a chair before her legs gave way, and covered her face with her hands. Luke had virtually ignored her for the past three weeks and yet he'd only had to touch her and she'd responded with a passion that was both terrifying and humiliating. Tentatively she touched her swollen lips with the tip of her tongue, and cringed inwardly, her eyes clouding with self-condemnation. What had happened to her pride? Her self-respect? She'd betrayed herself completely tonight... She might just as well have shouted out her love for Luke over the Tannoy. Oh, God, how could she have been so weak, so mindless...?

'Is there a time on the Guernsey?'

Vaguely she registered the airport luggage hand standing in the doorway, looking at her questioningly.

'Yes. The aircraft's just called in,' she told him quickly. 'ETA about five minutes.'

She forced herself to her feet, slipped on the uniform coat she'd borrowed earlier in the day from one of the cabin crew, and followed the overalled figure down the corridor.

* * *

Mike waited until the last passenger had collected his suitcase from the baggage hall and then reluctantly began to retrace her steps back to the Kingston Air offices, wishing desperately that she could simply go straight to the car park and drive home to the sanctity of Rakers' Moon. She dreaded having to face Luke again tonight. She felt too vulnerable, her nerves raw and as taut as a steel wire. Deliberately she schooled her features into a blank, impassive mask and then wondered why she was even bothering with the subterfuge. Wasn't it a little late to assume such pretended indifference to Luke?

She found him in the operations-room seated at one of the desks, his dark head bent over a pile of paperwork. Silently she entered the office and hung up her coat, watching him all the while from under her lashes.

She licked her dry lips. 'Is there anything I can do to help?' she addressed the lean back, her voice calm and controlled.

'No, thanks, Mike.' He flicked her a glance over his shoulder. 'I should be finished in a couple of minutes.'

'If it's all right, I may as well go straight on home, then,' she said briskly, picking up her handbag, relieved that this ordeal wasn't going to be prolonged any further.

Her relief was short-lived as Luke suddenly flung back his chair. 'No, it damn well isn't all right!' he thundered, his eyes blazing at her. 'You're not leaving this room until I've had a few straight answers.' Swiftly he crossed the floor and stood towering over her. 'What the hell's been the matter with you these last few weeks?' His hands closed over her shoulders like a steel clamp, holding her immobile.

'I don't know what you mean,' Mike said weakly, finding it difficult to meet his gaze.

'Don't you? Three weeks ago I spent the day in the company of a beautiful, warm, caring, responsive woman.' The anger had drained from his face. His voice was soft, caressing her as he'd earlier caressed her with his mouth and hands. 'That evening I had to go to Geneva.' He paused, and Mike jolted as his hands dropped to her waist, her pulses beginning to beat erratically. 'On my return I found a cold, impersonal stranger.'

Shock waves tingled down her spine. *She* was the one responsible for the coolness that had existed between them over the past weeks. It wasn't Luke who had changed—but her. She might have told herself that she was prepared to risk a casual liaison with him, but it had all been bravado and deep down she'd shied away from the very thought. Subconsciously she'd erected a protective, defensive barrier around her, deliberately trying to shut Luke out both mentally and physically.

'At first I thought you were sulking because I'd been forced to cancel our dinner date that evening.'

'That's absolutely ridiculous,' she denied hotly.

'Is it?' His head was bent towards her, his breath warm against her cheek.

Mike swallowed, mustering every ounce of self-control. 'D-didn't it ever occur to you that I simply didn't want to become involved with you any further?' Her heart was pounding so loudly that he must surely hear it.

'Yes, it did.' He touched her forehead with his lips. 'And that's why I kept my distance.' His mouth brushed over her cheekbones. 'But I don't believe that's true any more. Look at me, Mike,' he demanded hoarsely, 'and tell me you want me to leave you alone.'

She gave an involuntary gasp of shock as he eased her blouse from the waistband of her skirt and his fingers seared her naked flesh, moving in a slow, sensual rhythm across her back.

'This isn't fair,' she choked, shivering as his hand slid round to her rib-cage and then curved around the swell of her breast.

'And have you been fair to me?' he muttered thickly, his lips trailing a scalding path down her throat. 'Do you know what it's like seeing you every day, wanting to hold you, to touch you . . . and watching you flinch every time I come anywhere near you . . .?' He crushed her against him, his face fierce with desire, his eyes dark, heavy with need.

'Luke,' Mike said frantically, feeling her own control slipping away, her suppliant body melting into the hard, male frame. 'Someone might come in . . .'

'Come back to my cottage.'

'No! I can't . . . I don't want to . . .'

'Stop pretending.' Luke's mouth was against her ear, his tongue teasing the sensitive spot beneath it. 'You want me to make love to you as much as I want to. Admit it, Mike. You can't run away forever.'

'I . . .' It was pointless to deny it, nor was she going to be able to resist him for much longer, she thought desperately. Summoning all her strength, she pushed against the hard wall of his chest, and jerked herself free of his restraining arms, hastily tucking her blouse back into her skirt. 'I don't want a casual affair with you. I c-couldn't deal with it.'

'There is nothing casual about my feelings for you,' he rasped harshly. There was a leap of anger in his eyes. 'What the hell do you think I'm proposing? A one-night stand?' Abruptly, he turned away and walked over to the window and stood staring out into the darkness.

Uncertainly, Mike moved towards him. 'Luke?'

He looked down at her with frozen eyes. 'You may as well go home,' he dismissed her curtly. 'I'll lock up.'

'OK.' She felt as if she'd been slapped in the face. She collected her belongings and then paused in the doorway. 'Goodnight, Luke.'

He had resumed his stance by the window, and if he heard her he gave no indication of it. Mike's face tightened. He'd accused her of sulking earlier, she recalled. Wasn't that exactly what he was now doing, simply because she'd declined to go back to the cottage with him? Throwing a scornful look at his back, she closed the door and walked swiftly down the corridor, through the empty terminal and out into the cool night air.

She took a deep breath and began to walk towards the car park. She'd won a battle with herself tonight, she supposed, but she felt no sense of victory. Her hands, thrust deep into the pockets of her jacket, clenched into tight fists. She wanted to scream, to burst into tears, to bang her head against a brick wall...anything to relieve that twisted, aching feeling gnawing inside her.

She fished into her handbag for her car keys, unlocked the door of the Porsche and slipped into the driver's seat. She was just about to turn on the ignition when the car phone buzzed. Her immediate reaction was to ignore it, but it continued to ring insistently and unenthusiastically she reached out a hand and picked up the receiver.

'Hello?'

'Mike?'

Even though she'd half guessed it would be Luke, the sound of the deep voice still caught her off guard, made her heart skip a painful beat.

'Are you still in the car park?'

She inclined her head.

'Are you nodding or shaking your head?' he enquired drily.

'I'm still in the car park,' she said coolly, in no mood to share the amusement in his voice.

'Good.' There was a long pause. 'We need to talk.'

'I suppose so,' she admitted reluctantly. They couldn't continue as if nothing had happened tonight. The tension between them at work tomorrow would be unendurable. 'Shall I come back over to the office?' she asked uneasily.

'No. If I see you again tonight, I'm not going to be able stop myself from making love to you.'

The blood rushed to her head and a tremor passed through her body. He didn't even have to touch her, she thought resentfully, to evoke a response from her. He could seduce her with words alone and the mental image they conjured up.

'I'm in love with you, Mike.'

'What?' she muttered incredulously. Had she heard correctly? He sounded so calm, so matter of fact, as unemotional as if he were relaying the latest weather forecast. Was this his idea of a joke? She needed to see his face, needed to see the expression in his eyes...

'You intrigued me from the start.' His voice was huskier now. 'But falling in love with you was the last thing I intended to do. I didn't even realise that I was until the day I collected you from Heathrow, and by then it was already too late to do anything about it. I was a hopeless case.'

'You realised you loved me the afternoon I was nearly sick all over you?' Mike felt a mounting hysteria.

'Who said the age of romance was dead?' he murmured and vividly she pictured his face, could almost see his grin. 'You suddenly seemed so vulnerable. I found myself wanting to protect you...take care of you...' There was a catch in his voice and suddenly all Mike's doubts vanished.

He loved her. She gazed wildly around her, the adrenalin pumping through her. *Luke Duncan loved her.*

'Why...why...?' She stopped, swallowed hard and tried again. 'Why didn't you tell me this just now?'

'Because you wouldn't have believed me,' he said quietly. 'You'd have thought it was just a line to persuade you to share my bed for the night.'

Would she have thought that? Perhaps she might have initially, Mike admitted, although deep down instinct would have told her that Luke would never resort to such despicable tactics with any woman.

'I'm going up to Manchester tomorrow on the early evening flight and staying overnight. I'd like you to come with me.' He paused. 'And stop pursing your lips,' he admonished teasingly. 'I'm going to visit my parents.'

'You want me to meet them?'

'I want you to be part of my life, Mike, and that includes my family,' he said quietly. 'You will come, won't you?' There was a note of uncharacteristic hesitation in the deep voice.

'Yes.' Curiosity alone would have compelled her to accompany him.

'Drive home carefully. Goodnight, Mike.'

Dazedly, she replaced the receiver and stared down at it. Was she going insane? Had Luke actually called her up on the car phone and told her he loved her? A bubble of laughter welled up in her throat. A car park was hardly the most romantic of settings in which to receive a proposal! She flinched the moment the words formed in her head, her whole body stiffening. Luke hadn't mentioned marriage, she told herself fiercely, appalled by her unconscious blunder. He hadn't once referred to the future or suggested any permanent commitment. Neither, she reminded himself, had he even asked if she reciprocated his feelings.

She drew a long, deep breath and slumped back in her seat. For pity's sake, what was the matter with her? Luke had told her he loved her. What more did she want?

But for how long would he love her? The tortuous doubts crept insidiously into her mind. Were Luke's feelings as transitory as her father's, who fell in and out of love with monotonous regularity, and each time with a younger woman? She mustn't keep comparing the two men, she thought uneasily... but they were so alike. Throughout her life, she'd witnessed women's reaction to her father, a reaction that seemed to be magnified in Luke's case. Her throat tightened. She couldn't bear it if she was just a passing infatuation, couldn't bear to have been loved by Luke and then lose him to another woman.

'I want you to be part of my life.' His words reverberated through her head. That was the fundamental difference between them. Despite her repeated avowals to the contrary, she knew with dreary certainty that Luke would form the nucleus of her entire existence. She would love him to the exclusion of everyone and anything else. But she would only ever fill a small slot in his life, would always be competing for his time with the ever increasing demands of his business empire. And inevitably she would be the loser.

The tap at the window made her start, and, turning her head swiftly, Mike saw the dark figure looming over the car. Without thinking, governed solely by instinct and driving need, she flung open the car door and launched herself into Luke's arms.

Their bodies and mouths fused together, passion flaring instantly and mounting into a burning inferno that threatened to engulf them completely.

Mike moaned a throaty protest as Luke dragged his mouth from hers, and eased her arms from around his neck.

'I want you, Mike.' A shudder passed through the muscular length. 'But I want you without any reservations.'

So he had guessed at those tortuous doubts that had assailed her, knew about that deep well of insecurity. Slowly, Mike raised her eyes to his, and in the dark grey shadowy depths read the question being asked of her. With all her heart she longed to tell him that she trusted him implicitly, that she loved him unequivocally...but she couldn't do it. The words stuck in the throat. No longer able to meet his intense gaze, she lowered her head unhappily.

'Get back into your car and drive home before I change my mind.' The strain on his face was reflected in the gruffness of his voice as he pushed her away from him and walked with uncharacteristic jerkiness across the car park.

*   *   *

'How far are we from the centre of Manchester?' Mike asked as Luke drove the hire car they'd collected on their arrival at Ringway Airport through a small, picturesque village.

'Just a few miles.'

'Good heavens,' she murmured wonderingly, gazing out of the window. 'But it's so quiet and peaceful.'

'What were you expecting? A huge, industrial sprawl?' Luke was clearly amused by her surprise. 'The Peak District, which has some of wildest country in Britain, is only a short drive away. I used to cycle over there at weekends when I was a boy.'

The fields gave way to urban development as they reached the outskirts of Altrincham where Luke had told her his parents lived. Not normally apprehensive about meeting strangers, Mike was disconcerted to discover that she was beginning to feel quite sick with nerves.

Luke drove along a wide, tree-lined avenue and swung into the drive of a pleasant, red-bricked house, set back from the road in what appeared to be extensive grounds.

'Relax,' he murmured quietly as he helped Mike from the car. 'My parents rarely eat guests on Thursdays.'

Before Mike had time to inform him coolly that she wasn't in the least bit nervous, the front door was flung open and a golden Labrador tore down the path, greeted them rapturously, and hurtled around the side of the house. A slight woman, her light brown hair streaked with grey, followed more sedately, shadowed by a black and white border collie.

She hugged Luke and then, after he'd made a brief introduction, kissed Mike unceremoniously on the cheek, the warmth radiating from her deep blue eyes making formal words of welcome unnecessary.

'Come on in.' She linked her arm through Mike's and guided her into the house, the collie trailing faithfully behind them. 'We're having a drink on the terrace before dinner as it's such a lovely evening. Lisa is here, too, by the way,' she added over her shoulder to Luke who was following with the two overnight cases. 'She's making a guest appearance in that detective series they film up in the Dales.'

Mike had a brief impression of a wide, airy hall before being led through a large, comfortable lounge and out through open french windows on to a patio, bathed in evening sunshine.

'Peter, darling, this is Michaelia.'

Mike's eyes were riveted to the tall, grey-haired man who, after gently tipping a small tortoiseshell cat from his lap, rose to his feet courteously and extended a lean, tanned hand towards her.

'How do you do, Mr Duncan?' The resemblance between father and son was almost uncanny. The lines etched around the dark grey eyes and firm mouth of the older man merely added even more character to the rugged, compelling face. It was as if she were seeing Luke as he would look in thirty years' time.

'I believe you've already met my niece, Lisa?'

'Yes.' Mike exchanged smiles with the fair woman lounging elegantly in a wicker chair, rather wishing she could obliterate the memory of their first encounter from her mind, and wondering a little uneasily just how much Luke's parents knew about it.

'Hi, Lissy.' Luke walked across and kissed his cousin on the cheek. 'Tom not with you?'

Lisa shook her head regretfully. 'He was hoping to come down this weekend but he's pretty tied up at work.' She gave a light, not wholly convincing laugh. 'Do you know that in the six years Tom and I have been married, we've only actually spent about half of that time together? Either I'm away on location or he's out of the country on a business trip.'

'You must miss him,' Mike said sympathetically, sitting down beside her as the two men moved over to the drinks tray and Luke's mother, murmuring something about needing more ice, disappeared into the house, followed inevitably by the collie.

'I do. Desperately.' Lisa sighed. 'But even if I gave up acting, we'd still spend weeks and weeks apart while Tom was abroad.' She took a sip from her glass and surveyed Mike thoughtfully over the rim. 'I suppose that you and Luke are going to be in much the same position. Or do you intend to travel with him and spend half your life living out of a suitcase and waiting around in strange hotels?'

'I . . . That is, we haven't actually . . .' Mike floundered to a stop, at a total loss at how to answer the question. She wasn't even certain she had a future with Luke, let alone knew what form it might take. Her embarrassment increased as she was suddenly aware that Luke had rejoined them and must have overheard Lisa's last words and her own stumbling attempt at a reply. Cautiously she flicked him a glance, dismayed by the coolness in his eyes. He was angry . . .

'What would you like to drink, Mike?' he asked expressionlessly. 'Wine? Or there's some home-made lemonade if you would prefer it?'

'That sounds lovely,' she answered brightly, immeasurably relieved as Luke's mother emerged from the house and the conversation became general. Luke, she noticed with growing unease, took little part in it but sat motionless in his chair, his eyes dark and remote. Was he regretting bringing her here with him? she wondered unhappily.

'I expect you'd like to freshen up before dinner,' Luke's mother murmured gently. 'I'll show you where your room is.'

'I'll take Michaelia upstairs,' Lisa offered, rising to her feet in a swift, elegant movement, and implanting a swift kiss on the top of her aunt's head as she passed. They were a very affectionate, tactile family, Mike mused, wondering how it would feel to really belong to such a warm unit.

'Be careful of Tilly as you go up, dear.'

Tilly turned out to be large tabby cat curled up in a large somnolent ball halfway up the stairs. Mike stooped to stroke her, was rewarded with an appreciative purr, and then hastily followed Lisa on up to the landing.

'Here you are,' Lisa announced opening the door into a small, attractively decorated and furnished bedroom. 'Bathroom's first on the left.'

'What a beautiful garden.' Mike was drawn to the window that overlooked the large grounds at the rear of the house. Below her, Luke's parents were strolling arm in arm across the lawn, talking animatedly together.

'They've been virtually inseparable for over forty years and yet they never seem to run out of things to say to each other,' Lisa murmured, peering over Mike's shoulder. Her eyes softened as they rested on her aunt. 'She gave up her career for him, you know. Apparently she was quite a brilliant musician and had a glittering future ahead of her. And then she came up to Manchester to give a concert, met Uncle Peter and they were married a month later.'

Mike frowned. It might sound incredibly romantic—but what an appalling waste of talent. 'Surely she could have combined a career with marriage?'

'I don't think she could bear the thought of being parted from my uncle when she went on concert tours.' Lisa smiled. 'My aunt doesn't exactly give the impression of being a frustrated woman suffering from burning regrets, does she?'

'No,' Mike agreed slowly. Luke's mother was one of the most serenely content persons she'd ever met. 'I suppose Luke inherited her talent.'

'You've heard him play the piano?' Lisa sat down on the edge of the bed, watching as Mike began to unpack her overnight case.

'Only once,' Mike admitted, hanging up her bathrobe.

'He was one of those nauseating child prodigies. The type that can play Chopin with their eyes closed before they can even walk.' She grinned. 'Maybe I'm exaggerating a bit, but he really was exceptionally gifted.'

'So why did he give it up?'

'Didn't he tell you?' Lisa surveyed Mike curiously, making the latter acutely aware of just how little she knew about the man she loved. 'He broke three fingers on his right hand when he was at the Royal College of Music and that virtually put paid to any chance he might have had of being a top concert pianist. It was such a stupid accident too. He slammed his hand in a car door.' Lisa's eyes darkened reminiscently. 'He was very cut up about it, but, of course, being Luke, he wouldn't even talk about it.'

Mike's heart constricted with pain, finding it almost unbearable to have to imagine Luke's mental suffering.

'Then one day he just calmly announced that he was going to America and the next thing we knew he was on his way to making his first million.' Lisa stood up. 'It's odd how life turns out, isn't it? When we were children, the last thing I'd have ever imagined Luke being was a successful business tycoon.' She walked across the room to the door. 'See you back downstairs.'

Mike nodded vaguely. Lisa was right. It was odd the way life turned out. If a completely avoidable accident hadn't prevented him from pursuing his initial choice of career, it was very doubtful that Luke's and her paths would have ever crossed. Whatever happened, however much pain she might ultimately have to endure, Mike suddenly thought fiercely, she would never regret meeting Luke, never regret loving him. Shaking herself mentally, she picked up one of the towels laid out for her on the bed and headed for the bathroom.

Not wishing to be late for dinner, she had a quick wash, brushed her hair and swiftly reapplied her lipstick. Feeling fresher, she started to make her way back downstairs, pausing en route to stroke the tabby cat again who was still sprawled lazily on the stairs. Hearing the sound of voices from below her, she glanced over the banisters and saw Luke and Lisa emerge from the living-room and walk across the hall.

'You still haven't been down to the Cotswolds to see our cottage.'

Mike smiled slightly at the admonishing tone in Lisa's clear voice.

'Tom and I are hoping to go down there next weekend. Why don't you and Michaelia come then?'

'Sorry, Lissy,' Luke murmured regretfully, opening the door of the dining-room and standing aside to let her enter first. 'I'll be in the States then. I'm flying back to New York next Tuesday.'

Mike's knuckles whitened as they clutched hold of the banisters, her whole body shaking with shocked anger.

CHAPTER EIGHT

'MORE coffee, Michaelia?'

'No, thank you.' Mike smiled across the lounge to where Luke's mother was seated on a large leather settee beside her husband, presiding over a silver coffee-pot. Did this warm, charming woman have any idea of what a loathsome, devious, selfish swine she had for a son?

Mike's face was beginning to ache with the effort of maintaining that forced, bright smile. Somehow she'd managed to get through dinner, which, judging from the appreciative comments around her, had been excellent although she herself hadn't tasted any of it. She'd spent most of the time gazing down at her plate, concentrating on avoiding Luke's enquiring glances, knowing that if she looked at him directly she would probably explode and disgrace herself completely.

'Another brandy?' Peter Duncan rose to his feet and moved across the russet carpet to a large, old-fashioned sideboard on which were arrayed several decanters.

Mike refused politely, conscious of Luke's dark eyes resting on her face. She had sensed his amazement when she'd not only accepted a brandy with her first coffee, but had then tossed it back recklessly in one long gulp, miraculously managing to avoid choking as it burnt the back of her throat. However, instead of having the calming effect she'd hoped for, it had been like throwing petrol on to a bonfire and had simply refuelled the anger scorching through her.

Her gaze rested momentarily on the tall, grey-haired man. Why couldn't Luke have resembled his father in character as well as physical appearance? She had witnessed the tenderness in Peter Duncan's eyes as they followed his wife's every movement. A warm, caring, considerate man. Totally unlike his son. Instinctively Mike glanced towards Luke, and saw his dark eyebrows knit together as he met her icy glare.

'Anyone feel like a breath of fresh air?' Rising abruptly to his feet, he addressed the room at large, but Mike was fully aware that the invitation had been directed at her.

'Count me out.' Lisa stifled a yawn. 'I'm off to bed in a moment. The car's coming to collect me at the crack of dawn.'

'Mike?' Luke towered above her. 'Fancy a walk?'

The Labrador stretched out on the hearthrug sat up instantly it heard the magical, canine word, its tail wagging furiously. In contrast, the black and white collie crouched protectively by his mistress's feet made it quite evident that nothing would induce him to desert his post.

'Yes, why not?' Mike murmured casually and saw Luke's parents exchange glances. What were they envisaging? she wondered wryly. A romantic stroll in the moonlight? 'I'll just fetch my jacket.'

Luke was waiting for her in the hall when she returned, the Labrador straining at the lead held in his hand. Wordlessly, he opened the front door and Mike followed him down the drive.

Neither of them uttered a sound as they strode along the pavement, clearly illuminated by the street lamps and full moon. How long did Luke intend to keep up this war of silent attrition? Mike wondered disdainfully, flicking him a glance, her eyes resting on the tenacious angle of the uncompromising jaw. She was totally unaware of the equally stubborn set of her own small chin.

Turning left abruptly at the end of the street, Luke led her along another seemingly endless road, until they reached an area of open common ground, surrounded by trees. Released from its lead, the Labrador bounded ahead, dived into a clump of bushes, and returned proudly bearing a large stick which it lay carefully at Luke's feet.

Stooping down, Luke picked up the stick and hurled it with all his strength across the grass.

'Right,' he rasped, turning to Mike. 'What the hell is this all about?'

She didn't even pretend to misunderstand him. She was past playing games. 'I overheard you telling Lisa that you were going back to New York next week.' Her eyes blazed up at him. 'You might have damn well told me first. I'm your business partner if nothing else.'

'You're more than that and you know it,' he grated back. 'I was going to tell you——'

'When? On the morning of your departure?' she cut through bitterly.

'Tonight. I was waiting until you'd met my parents.'

She looked at him uncomprehendingly, unable to make the connection, and then gave up trying as he took hold of her hands.

'I want you to come with me.'

She stiffened. 'To New York? What for? A vacation?' she demanded caustically.

'My God, you can be aggravating,' he thundered. 'You know perfectly well what for. I want you to be with me. I want to wake up in the mornings and find you beside me.'

Mike's heart thudded against her rib-cage, a misty image floating blissfully into her head of herself and Luke, lying, arms entwined, in a huge bed. And then the idyllic picture faded, harsh reality sweeping it aside. The reality would be her alone in some huge, modern New York apartment, filling in her days with aimless pursuits, waiting for the moment when she heard Luke's key in the door... waiting for the inevitable telephone calls from his secretary to say that he'd been delayed in a board meeting... waiting for him to return from some overseas business trip. Waiting. Always waiting. Just as her numerous stepmothers had waited for her father—until they'd finally grown tired of the excuses, tired of always being placed last in the list of priorities.

Mike's throat constricted. It would be all too easy to say yes, to throw caution to the wind. But she mustn't weaken, mustn't give up her independence to become a mere temporary appendage to Luke's life. It was far too dangerous a trap to fall into. One day, she thought bleakly, she would wake up and find herself with nothing.

'You seem to have conveniently forgotten about Kingston Air.' She finally found her voice.

'Steven Evans is more than capable of running it on a day-to-day basis.'

'Oh, I'm fully aware that I'm not indispensable,' she flashed back. 'But hasn't it ever occurred to you that I might happen to enjoy working at the airport... that I might actually have some plans of my own for KA?' Inspiration struck. 'Like expanding the engineering section, so that we can deal with more than just routine maintenance.' Why had she never thought of that before? 'And what about Rakers' Moon? My family?' Had he stopped for even one second to consider what he was asking her to give up for an uncertain future with him?

'We could always get married if that's what you want.'

Mike stared at him incredulously as she registered the complete and utter indifference in his voice as he made what was presumably a proposal. His attitude to marriage was as casual as her father's, she thought disbelievingly. 'You haven't listened to one word I've been saying,' she said quietly. Did Luke really think that was all she wanted? A gold band and a piece of paper that her father had proved was utterly meaningless?

'Mike...' The sudden urgency in his voice alerted her to his intention and she averted her face quickly so that his mouth missed her lips and brushed past her ear.

'There has to be more to a relationship than...this.' She tugged her hands free from his clasp. 'At least for me.' She swallowed hard. 'No, Luke,' she said quietly. 'I don't want to go to New York with you.'

A cloud scudded across the moon, making it impossible to see the expression on his face, but when he finally spoke his voice was even and completely controlled.

'Normally, I'd suggest that we take the first flight back in the morning, but...'

She nodded in silent agreement. His parents were expecting them to stay until the evening. An earlier abrupt departure would necessitate awkward explanations, and she didn't want to run the risk of offending the couple who had welcomed her with such warmth into their home. She'd managed to get through this evening, Mike thought resolutely. Somehow she'd survive tomorrow.

* * *

Mike gazed out of the small oval window, the runway landing lights stretching out below as the aircraft began its final approach into the familiar airfield. Wincing slightly, she closed her eyes for a second and pressed her fingers to her temple.

'Headache?' Luke asked quietly. He'd spent most of the flight up in the cockpit, only returning to his seat beside her when the aircraft started its descent.

'Just a bit. Probably too much sun,' she dismissed it lightly, knowing full well that the throbbing pain in her head hadn't been caused by the May sunshine.

Accompanied by his parents, they'd spent the day walking in the Dales, under a clear, dazzling blue sky. In any other circumstances, she thought ruefully, the day would have been perfect. But she'd been far too tense to truly appreciate the breathtakingly beautiful scenery around her.

She'd been totally bewildered by Luke's attitude towards her. She'd been apprehensive about facing him again this morning, had been prepared for at least a period of initial awkwardness between them. But when she'd walked into the dining-room for breakfast Luke had greeted her with a casual cheerfulness that spoke of a long, untroubled night's sleep. While she'd only managed a slice of toast—untruthfully assuring his mother that she seldom ate more than that in the morning—Luke had worked his way through a large cooked breakfast. At first she'd wondered if his apparent good humour was merely an act for his parents' benefit, but it had persisted even when they were alone. He had treated her with unfailing courtesy throughout the day, and with a relaxed friendliness she found impossible to reciprocate.

She simply couldn't understand him, found his behaviour incomprehensible. Never once did he refer to the previous night. It was as if he'd simply wiped out the last two days from his mind. Her rejection hadn't even touched his male ego, let alone caused any more lasting emotional wounds. Finally, Mike came to the conclusion that his feelings for her were even more transitory and superficial than she'd supposed initially. In five days' time he would be flying back to New York; in a week, maybe two, she thought bitterly, he would have probably forgotten her very existence.

The aircraft taxied to a halt and Mike unfastened her safety-belt and followed Luke down the aisle to the rear passenger door.

'I'm going to call in the office and check up on any messages for me,' Luke announced as they walked across the tarmac towards the passenger terminal.

Mike looked at him disbelievingly. Did work monopolise his every waking thought? After breakfast that morning he'd put through a lengthy call to his London office.

'Hope your headache gets better soon,' he added casually, turning away from her.

'Thank you,' she returned politely, heading in the opposite direction towards the car park. It wasn't until she was almost back at Rakers' Moon that she realised she'd forgotten to collect her overnight bag from the aircraft. She'd pick it up in the morning, she decided, and frowned as she saw the familiar bright red sports car drawn up in front of Rakers' Moon. What on earth was Christina doing here?

She discovered her half-sister in the drawing-room, reclining gracefully on the sofa, watching the television.

'Mike!' Christina greeted her enthusiastically and then explained, 'I phoned last night to ask if I could come down for the weekend and John said you wouldn't be back until tonight. So I thought I'd come on down anyway today and surprise you. You don't mind, do you?' Without giving Mike a chance to reply, she continued, 'I've brought Oliver with me, too.'

'Have you?' Mike said delightedly. 'Where is he?'

'He wanted to wait up until you arrived, and I thought a late night wouldn't hurt him for once, but he fell asleep on the sofa so I popped him up to bed. He's in the room next to yours.' Christina paused for breath. 'I'd forgotten just how huge Rakers' Moon is. You must get awfully lonely rattling around here on your own.'

'John and Ellen live in, don't forget,' Mike murmured and swiftly changed the subject. 'What time did you arrive?'

'About six. I haven't had supper yet. Ellen's left a casserole in the oven and I told her we'd just help ourselves. Is that all right?'

'Of course.' Impulsively, Mike hugged the younger girl, relieved to find her in such good spirits, remembering how downcast Christina had appeared when she'd last seen her. 'It's so lovely to see you,' she said warmly. 'I've been meaning to ask you down for ages,' she added guiltily, 'but...' But she'd been too occupied with her own life, she realised with burning shame.

Christina didn't seem to notice Mike's hesitation. 'I've something important to tell you——' she announced, her dark eyes shining with excitement.

'Tell you what,' Mike interrupted, knowing from past experience just how long her half-sister took to impart any of her news. 'Just let me dash upstairs, have a quick shower and change out of this suit, and then we'll have supper on our laps in here, and have a good long chat.'

She bounded out of the room and up the stairs, feeling happier than she had for days, aware too that her headache seemed to have eased. Unable to resist the temptation, she tiptoed into the bedroom next to hers, and stood for a moment gazing down at the sleeping small boy. Christina had been right, she admitted honestly. She did get lonely living in Rakers' Moon on her own. It was a house designed for a large family. It needed to be filled with children—and with cats and dogs, she added with a smile, thinking of Luke's parents. Silently she crept out of the room and made her way to her own bedroom.

After a quick shower, she dressed in a pair of comfortable, faded jeans and a huge, shapeless jumper that should have been discarded years ago, but to which she'd become deeply attached. Winding a towel around her damp hair, she returned downstairs, thinking how blissful it was to be able to relax at long last.

'Shall I start dishing up?' she began as she walked into the drawing-room and then paused in dismay. Luke was sitting on the sofa beside Christina, looking completely at home.

'You forgot your case,' Christina said cheerfully, seemingly completely oblivious to the frozen expression on her half-sister's face. 'Luke dropped it off on his way home, so I asked him to stay for supper. There's loads for three.'

'I see,' Mike said stiffly, conscious of the dark grey eyes assessing her scruffy appearance. 'Right, if everyone's ready, we might as well have it.' How dared Christina invite Luke to supper without consulting her first? And why hadn't he had the tact to refuse the invitation?

'I'll come and help you,' Christina offered, following Mike into the kitchen. 'You didn't mind me asking Luke, did you?'

'Of course not,' Mike said airily. 'Why should I?' She opened the oven door, lifted out the casserole dish and began to spoon the contents on to three plates.

'There's not much on this one,' Christina murmured helpfully.

'It's mine. I'm not very hungry.' Mike placed two generously laden plates on a tray and handed it to the other girl. 'Yours and Luke's. Take them on through. I'll bring the cutlery.' She wasn't going to alter her initial plan to eat supper on their laps just because Luke was here, she thought determinedly. Neither was she going to rush upstairs and change out of her disreputable, ill-fitting jumper. And the turban could remain where it was until her hair was dry. After all, she hadn't asked Luke to stay for supper. He wasn't her guest. Abruptly she snatched the towel from her head. Well, her hair was almost dry...

As she entered the drawing-room, she found Luke and Christina engaged in a light, bantering conversation.

'Knives and forks,' Mike announced, letting them clatter noisily on to a coffee-table.

'Thanks,' Luke murmured politely, giving her little more than a cursory glance before turning his full attention back to Christina.

Slumping down on a chair, Mike began to eat mechanically, watching the expression of amusement pass over Luke's face as Christina began to tease him with a familiarity that was indicative of more than just casual acquaintance. All those business trips to

London which Luke had undertaken over the past few weeks...had he seen Christina on each occasion? Mike pushed her knife and fork together and stood up.

'I'm going to bed.'

At least her curt announcement seemed to remind Luke of her existence, she thought bitterly, as he turned his dark head towards her.

'Still have that headache?' he enquired blandly.

'Yes,' she lied swiftly.

'Mike, I didn't realise. You should have said something.' Christina was instantly sympathetic. 'Take some aspirin,' she advised.

'I expect an early night should do the trick,' Mike said briskly, moving across the room. She paused in the doorway and glanced back over her shoulder. Luke and Christina had forgotten her already, and were once again completely absorbed in conversation—and each other.

Preparing quickly for bed, Mike slipped in between the sheets, and leaving the bedside lamp on stared up at the ceiling. She was jealous of Christina, her own half-sister, she admitted with self-disgust. And she had no right to be. She had absolutely no claim on Luke. It was time she accepted that whatever relationship she'd had with him was well and truly over. She'd been perfectly happy before she'd met him, she reminded herself forcefully, and she would be again. She didn't need a man—and especially not Luke Duncan—to make her life complete. From now on, she thought resolutely, she would concentrate all her energies on Kingston Air.

She frowned as she heard the light tap on her door. 'Come in,' she muttered unenthusiastically.

Christina walked in, looking a little uncertain. 'I saw your light was still on. Are you feeling any better?'

'Yes, thanks. Has Luke gone already?' she asked with assumed uninterest and, seeing Christina's nod of confirmation, added carefully, 'You and he seem to get on very well together.' Why, she wondered drearily, was she turning the knife in the wound like this?

'We do,' Christina agreed, sitting down on the edge of the bed. 'I've seen quite a lot of him recently,' she added casually, seemingly oblivious to Mike's frozen expression. 'He's been helping me . . .' She jumped to her feet. 'I shall explode if I don't tell you! Guess what? I'm going to train as a nurse.'

Mike sat bolt upright. 'When did you decide this?' she asked incredulously.

Christina paced over to the window. 'Do you remember when you had flu and I looked after you? Well, it was the first time I'd ever felt useful . . . felt needed.' She turned round to face Mike. 'And I suddenly realised that I wanted to do something with my life, not just sit around all day worrying about how I looked, waiting to get married.'

'Why didn't you tell me all this before?' Mike demanded and then winced. 'You did try to, didn't you? The day I went rushing down to the airport.' She had *known* something was troubling Christina, but she hadn't waited to find out what it was. Kingston Air had taken priority over her own half-sister. She'd been guilty of the very crime of which she'd accused both Luke and her father. It was an uncomfortable revelation. 'I'm sorry,' she muttered unhappily.

Christina shrugged. 'Anyway, the day after you left, Luke came up to London and took me out for lunch, and I told him about wanting to be a nurse. I thought he'd laugh, but he didn't. He was really interested and suggested I went to see a careers officer to find out all the details about training.' She smiled. 'He's been terrific, encouraged me all the way. Every time he came up to London on business, he used to pop in and see how I was getting on.' She took a deep breath. 'I know nursing is hard work,' she continued earnestly, 'and that I might be hopeless at it and not even finish my training. But at least I will have tried.'

'I think it's fantastic,' Mike said warmly, thinking how little she really knew about Christina. 'I suppose that's why you've seen so much of Luke,' she added slowly.

'Mmm.' Christina glanced at Mike's face and started to grin. 'You didn't think that Luke and I...?' She giggled. 'So that's why you've been in such a strange mood this evening. Oh, Mike, you idiot! I think Luke is wonderful. Who wouldn't? But he's too old for me, and, even if he weren't, I wouldn't stand a chance. Every time I see him, he spends half the time talking about you. I don't think he even knows he's doing it. He's absolutely crazy about you. Surely you know that?'

'He asked me to marry him,' Mike blurted out. 'And I refused.'

Christina sank down in a chair. 'Don't you love him?' she asked in amazement.

'Yes,' Mike mumbled. 'Isn't it ironic... you suddenly deciding you want a career?' She was beginning to feel slightly hysterical. 'And I'm supposed to be the one who's ambitious... and all I want is Luke.' Kingston Air didn't matter. She'd been deluding herself to think it did. Nothing mattered any more—except Luke.

'But if you love Luke, why——?' Christina shook her head in bafflement.

'Because it would never work,' Mike cut in drearily. 'Can't you see? Luke is just like Daddy. Maybe I'm selfish, but I want a husband I see every night and at weekends. I want my children to grow up knowing their father is always there if they need him.'

'Luke is nothing like Daddy,' Christina retorted fiercely. 'When I needed someone to talk to, who was it who made the time to listen? Not Daddy. Not even you. It was Luke. You're supposed to love him—and yet you don't know the first thing about him.'

'I've been such a fool.' Mike buried her face in her hands. She'd been so blind. Luke had warned her about leaping to conclusions about people—and she was still doing it. She'd misjudged Andrew Simpson, even Christina, and, worst of all, the man she loved. 'What am I going to do?' she muttered miserably. She was supposed to be the strong, confident, mature one, and here she was begging Christina for advice. 'I've so little time left to try and put things right. Luke's going back to New York on Tuesday.'

'Tuesday?' Christina exclaimed. 'But he told me tonight that he was catching a flight tomorrow morning from Heathrow because something urgent had just cropped up.'

'What?' Mike flung back the bedclothes and tugged on her jeans and jumper. He couldn't leave just like that, not without telling her, not without even saying goodbye.

'Mike, where are you going?'

'I have to see Luke before it's too late,' she muttered desperately, rushing to the door.

'But he's only...'

Christina's voice tailed off into the distance as she tore down the stairs.

*   *   *

The relief as she saw the light on in the cottage was overwhelming. She'd been terrified that Luke might have decided to go up to London tonight. As the Porsche squealed to a halt, Mike jumped out and ran up to the front door, hammering on it with her fist.

Oh, God, what was she doing here? She was going to make a complete fool of herself. Why hadn't she stopped to think before charging around here as if she were completely deranged? Luke didn't want her any more. He'd made that perfectly obvious. But it was too late to retreat now...the door was opening.

'Come to borrow some aspirin?' Luke drawled, leaning against the door-jamb.

'No...I...' Mike gazed up into the craggy face and swallowed hard. 'Christina said you were catching an earlier flight. Tomorrow. And I came to say...goodbye.' The tears were burning under her eyelids and she fought to control them. What did her pride matter? What did she have to lose? Except Luke. 'If you still want me to come to New York, I will. Not straight away, of course. I'll have to pack and...' Please say something, she implored him silently. Please put me out of this agony, one way or another.

'Why?' he demanded brusquely. 'Why have you changed your mind?'

'Because I love you,' she croaked. 'I don't care where we live as long as I'm with you. I don't care about Kingston Air any more. I'll sell Rakers' Moon.'

'That's entirely up to you. It's your house.'

'Yes,' she mumbled through frozen lips, her face ashen. That was her answer. Luke simply no longer cared about her.

'But I rather thought you might like to live there after we were married.'

Disbelievingly Mike searched his face, hope dawning as she saw the expression in his eyes that was at complete odds with the casualness in his voice.

With a muffled groan he pulled her into his arms. 'You will marry me, Mike, won't you?'

'Yes,' she said weakly, her eyes glowing. Wonderingly she reached up a hand and traced the contours of the strong, rugged face.

'And you really love me?'

'More than anything in the world,' she assured him softly, murmuring a blissful sigh as his mouth took possession of hers.

It was a long time before either of them spoke again and when Mike finally opened her eyes she found herself cradled in Luke's arms on the sofa in the sitting-room, although she had no real recollection of how she'd come to be there.

'You said something about living in Rakers' Moon after we were married,' she remembered hazily, nuzzling his neck. 'But I want to be wherever you are.'

Luke cupped her face with his hands, tilting it up towards him. 'I think I might have a small confession to make.' His eyes danced with teasing blue flames. 'I may have been guilty of misleading you again. I'm only going back to New York for a week. Ten days at most.'

'What?' Mike looked at him indignantly. 'And you deliberately let me think...' So that was what Christina had been trying to tell her when she'd rushed out of the house.

'You didn't think I was going to let you go that easily, did you?' He grinned, brushing her lips lightly. 'I'm in the process of selling my shares in Mereton Holdings. That's why I've been so damn busy the last few weeks, tearing about trying to organise everything. I've already resigned as chairman.'

Mike jerked herself upright. 'But you can't do that. Mereton Holdings is important to you.' One day he'd regret his decision, might even come to blame her for it.

'You're wrong,' he said quietly. 'Mereton Holdings has never been that important.' His mouth twisted. 'It's been a compensation, nothing more.'

For the loss of his musical career, Mike guessed at the words left unsaid, comprehension flooding her.

'And now I simply resent the demands it makes on my time,' he continued. 'From now on, I intend to concentrate on Kingston Air. And you.'

'Why didn't you tell me all this before?'

'I was going to, eventually, but I didn't want to rush things. Don't forget, I wasn't even certain that you loved me. I hoped you felt the same way about me— but I wasn't sure.' He smiled wryly. 'So I made my plan of campaign. I was going to come and live in England permanently, and do my damnedest to make you love me. I didn't care how long it took.' He sighed. 'The only reason I took you up to meet my parents is because I was trying to show you that, like them, I regarded marriage as a lifetime commitment.'

'And I overheard you telling Lisa you were going back to New York and thought——'

'I know exactly what you thought,' he mocked her.

'But you could have explained everything to me later,' she insisted.

'I was too damn angry with you to explain anything!'

'I'm sorry,' Mike said humbly.

'So you should be,' Luke teased her, kissing her soundly on the mouth. He lifted his head. 'Is Christina waiting up for you?'

'I think she'll guess where I am,' Mike mumbled, nestling into his arms contentedly.

'And if you don't arrive back until after breakfast tomorrow morning?' Luke queried, picking her up and carrying her towards the door.

'I think she might leap to the right conclusion.'

'You've just missed the turning.'

'I hope you're not going to turn into a nagging wife, Mrs Duncan.'

Mike giggled, brushing confetti from her hair. They were spending the first night of their married life at Rakers' Moon, and then tomorrow flying out to board a chartered yacht to spend four glorious weeks exploring the Greek Islands.

'Why are we stopping here?' she demanded as Luke helped her from the car.

'Patience, Mrs Duncan. And all will be revealed.' He opened the boot. 'Here you are.'

'A bucket and spade?' She was probably going to spend the rest of her life being married to a lunatic, Mike thought with an idiotic smile.

'This way. Follow me.'

'Are we going to Rakers' Pool?'

'Wait and see.'

'I love it when you're masterful.'

'Right. Close your eyes and count to ten, and when you open them imagine it's moonlight.'

'One...two...I can't kiss you and count at the same time,' Mike protested, opening her eyes, grinning as she saw the small metal container lying at the edge of the dewpond. 'Contraband!'

She picked up the tin, examined it curiously and flicked open the catch.

'What's this?' she frowned, extracting a typed document covered in a waterproof jacket.

'Half my shares in Kingston Air have been transferred to your name.'

Mike's eyes locked into Luke's. 'And, under the terms of Matthew's will, you now own half my shares. So that means we're still . . .'

'Partners.'

'Equal partners,' Mike reminded him solemnly and flung her arms around his neck. Equal partners for life.

 **Harlequin Presents**®

is

 exotic

 dramatic

 sensual

 exciting

 contemporary

 a fast, involving read

 terrific!!

Harlequin Presents—
passionate romances
around the world!

HARLEQUIN Romance®

HARLEQUIN ROMANCE
IS IN THE
WEDDING BUSINESS...

The August title in The Bridal Collection is about...
a wedding consultant!

THE BEST-MADE PLANS
by Leigh Michaels
Harlequin Romance #3214

THE BRIDAL COLLECTION

THE BRIDE arranged weddings.
The Groom avoided them.
Their own Wedding was ten years late!

Available in July in
The Bridal Collection:
BOTH OF THEM
by Rebecca Winters
Harlequin Romance #3210

Available wherever
Harlequin books are sold.

WED-4

WELCOME TO

The quintessential small town where everyone knows everybody else!

Finally, books that capture the pleasure of tuning in to your favorite TV show!

GREAT READING...GREAT SAVINGS...AND A FABULOUS FREE GIFT!

Each book set in Tyler is a self-contained love story; together, the twelve novels stitch the fabric of the community. The covers honor the old American tradition of quilting; each cover depicts a patch of the large Tyler quilt.

With Tyler you can receive a fabulous gift ABSOLUTELY FREE by collecting proofs-of-purchase found in each Tyler book. And use our special Tyler coupons to save on your next TYLER book purchase.

Join your friends at Tyler for the sixth book, SUNSHINE by Pat Warren, available in August.

When Janice Eber becomes a widow, does her husband's friend David provide more than just friendship?

"GET AWAY FROM IT ALL" SWEEPSTAKES

HERE'S HOW THE SWEEPSTAKES WORKS

NO PURCHASE NECESSARY

To enter each drawing, complete the appropriate Official Entry Form or a 3" by 5" index card by hand-printing your name, address and phone number and the trip destination that the entry is being submitted for (i.e., Caneel Bay, Canyon Ranch or London and the English Countryside) and mailing it to: Get Away From It All Sweepstakes, P.O. Box 1397, Buffalo, New York 14269-1397.

No responsibility is assumed for lost, late or misdirected mail. Entries must be sent separately with first class postage affixed, and be received by: 4/15/92 for the Caneel Bay Vacation Drawing, 5/15/92 for the Canyon Ranch Vacation Drawing and 6/15/92 for the London and the English Countryside Vacation Drawing. Sweepstakes is open to residents of the U.S. (except Puerto Rico) and Canada, 21 years of age or older as of 5/31/92.

For complete rules send a self-addressed, stamped (WA residents need not affix return postage) envelope to: Get Away From It All Sweepstakes, P.O. Box 4892, Blair, NE 68009.

© 1992 HARLEQUIN ENTERPRISES LTD.   SWP-RLS

"GET AWAY FROM IT ALL" SWEEPSTAKES

HERE'S HOW THE SWEEPSTAKES WORKS

NO PURCHASE NECESSARY

To enter each drawing, complete the appropriate Official Entry Form or a 3" by 5" index card by hand-printing your name, address and phone number and the trip destination that the entry is being submitted for (i.e., Caneel Bay, Canyon Ranch or London and the English Countryside) and mailing it to: Get Away From It All Sweepstakes, P.O. Box 1397, Buffalo, New York 14269-1397.

No responsibility is assumed for lost, late or misdirected mail. Entries must be sent separately with first class postage affixed, and be received by: 4/15/92 for the Caneel Bay Vacation Drawing, 5/15/92 for the Canyon Ranch Vacation Drawing and 6/15/92 for the London and the English Countryside Vacation Drawing. Sweepstakes is open to residents of the U.S. (except Puerto Rico) and Canada, 21 years of age or older as of 5/31/92.

For complete rules send a self-addressed, stamped (WA residents need not affix return postage) envelope to: Get Away From It All Sweepstakes, P.O. Box 4892, Blair, NE 68009.

© 1992 HARLEQUIN ENTERPRISES LTD.   SWP-RLS

"GET AWAY FROM IT ALL"

Brand-new Subscribers-Only Sweepstakes

OFFICIAL ENTRY FORM

This entry must be received by: **June 15, 1992**
This month's winner will be notified by: **June 30, 1992**
Trip must be taken between: July 31, 1992—July 31, 1993

YES, I want to win the vacation for two to England. I understand the prize includes round-trip airfare and the two additional prizes revealed in the BONUS PRIZES insert.

Name _____

Address _____

City _____

State/Prov._____ Zip/Postal Code_____

Daytime phone number _____
(Area Code)

Return entries with invoice in envelope provided. Each book in this shipment has two entry coupons — and the more coupons you enter, the better your chances of winning!
© 1992 HARLEQUIN ENTERPRISES LTD.   3M-CPN

"GET AWAY FROM IT ALL"

Brand-new Subscribers-Only Sweepstakes

OFFICIAL ENTRY FORM

This entry must be received by: **June 15, 1992**
This month's winner will be notified by: **June 30, 1992**
Trip must be taken between: July 31, 1992—July 31, 1993

YES, I want to win the vacation for two to England. I understand the prize includes round-trip airfare and the two additional prizes revealed in the BONUS PRIZES insert.

Name _____

Address _____

City _____

State/Prov._____ Zip/Postal Code_____

Daytime phone number _____
(Area Code)

Return entries with invoice in envelope provided. Each book in this shipment has two entry coupons — and the more coupons you enter, the better your chances of winning!
© 1992 HARLEQUIN ENTERPRISES LTD.   3M-CPN